PERIL, KENTUCKY

Peril, Kentucky

Joseph G. Anthony

WIND PUBLICATIONS

International Standard Book Number 1893239454
Library of Congress Control Number: 2005931651

First edition

Cover art: Woodcut by Dorothy L Mandel

To my wife, Elise, and to our children,

Sarah, David, Daniel: the ties that bind.

Chapter 1

"I hate this woman!!!" — the student's only comment.

Linda Eliot crouched a little lower in her almost new 1982 Tercel, being careful not to drip coffee onto her new lavender suit. She could just hear her mother. Such an impractical color, especially for a day filled with chalk dust. But she loved purple. And the tailored look toned down her figure, she thought, made her breasts look smaller. It had cost half her paycheck.

"I hate this woman!!!" She shook her head. What could she have possibly done to that student?

At 7 a.m., Peril Community College's back parking lot was the most private place in Linda's life. No students, no office mate. No Jimmy even. Mrs. Nelson often scolded her for being off alone—parked in such a secluded place, out of sight of the college. "You're a young woman, I don't care how educated you are," she'd say while giving Linda's office an extra mopping. But Linda felt perfectly safe.

Somebody had chopped the mountain with a cleaver, it appeared, in order to carve out the parking lot. The rock strata looked like the sliced epidermis in biology texts. Except that every third layer was black—coal. Fog circled the injured mountain like a giant smoke ring.

She turned to the next evaluation. They were from last semester, her first semester. It had taken the secretaries three months to type out the comments so the faculty wouldn't recognize the handwriting. She tried to picture the student as she read the comments but no face came to mind. How long could she last with comments like these?

1

"Don't worry about them," Jimmy told her. He had surprised her at six that morning, en route to Whitesburg to see a client. He had hoped to find her soft and sleepy, waking up only enough to give him a small smile as he slipped into her bed and wrapped the blankets and sheets around them. He imagined the smell of sweet sweat as they cacooned together, as he guided his body into hers when she was most receptive, before tension tightened her shoulders.

But she was already up when he arrived, staring out her kitchen window, already facing the day, already seeing him as one more person to deal with. She offered him coffee before she remembered. No caffeine. Not Jimmy. He sat with her, abandoning the idea of sex. "It was your first term. They'll get used to you. Hang on."

Hang on. Puddles from yesterday's rain were still pooled in the bare clay of the yard. She looked in the distance for the river but all she could see was a horizontal layer of fog. Only the tops of the trees were visible. They had just a hint of green. Three weeks until April. She was probably repeating all the things her students hated. But she didn't know what they were. She hadn't known they didn't like her. They were so polite, so full of smiles. Not like the Bronx, her only other teaching job, part time. Those students let you know right away if you stepped on their toes. Bronx cheers. She was a foreigner there, though it was only twenty minutes from her home. A white English speaking girl from Manhattan. She hadn't been making any difference to those students. Foreigner.

"It must be so different," everyone said to her. "New York and Kentucky."

"Not so different," she'd say. "Of course, parking's easier."

She breathed deeply and shivered a bit. The fog was lifting. Green shoots were poking their way through the brown grass. The patches of green that surrounded the small saplings were like clusters of refugees from winter. Smoke drifted in through the open window, smoke you could breathe, at least. She'd never been in a place where almost everybody smoked. Even at meetings.

"Shouldn't we be wearing one of those mining caps with a light?" she asked at one gathering. "The smoke's thick enough in here."

"Do you have asthma?" It was the only reason President Lowerly could imagine that someone would object to smoking.

"I'm getting it," she answered, and they had laughed as if the joke was the point, and kept on smoking.

Thank God, Jimmy didn't smoke. He took the Catholic rule of treating the body like a temple seriously, the only Catholic she knew who did.

"Sex allowed in your temple?" she had teased him. "Sounds more pagan than Catholic." He was pulling her away from her papers, down to the floor of her small living room. She wanted to suggest the bedroom but she knew they wouldn't make it there. She wished she had time to wash her hands, at least. They had red ink stains from her marking. But she didn't want to stop either.

"How do you think we got all those large families? No immaculate conceptions in my neighborhood." He had rolled her out of her blouse and bra in three smooth clicks of his fingers. Catholic boys, she knew, learned to move quickly. He paused before the sight of her breasts swinging in the half light of her desk lamp. He always paused. Grateful. Catholic boys might be quick, she remembered, but they were usually grateful.

Weren't they married, those begetters of large families? she wanted to quip, but stopped herself. She didn't need Jimmy on the subject of marriage. She nuzzled her lips into his shoulder to keep herself quiet while he slid her panties off. She opened her legs. She looked over his shoulders while he entered her. Her inky fingers pressed into his back and left red smudges.

At least nobody else said they hated her. She rested the evaluations on the leather steering wheel, a tacky feature, like the rainbow stripes on the car's sides. But it was what they'd had on the sales lot in Prestonsburg. It was either take the tacky features, pay extra for them, or wait for other cars that might or might not come in. Pay extra for tacky. That seemed the rule in the county. Suddenly she could picture the student who hated her, a mousy kind of girl with hair that hung over her face in twenty separate strands. Linda had almost told her about a cream she used that might help her bad skin, but the girl had never invited that kind of comment. Small breasts. Short. "I just don't know what you want!" the girl had spit out after getting a D on her third draft. What did she want? Just some intelligence, she should have told her. Just some originality. She did tell her to take it back and try again but the girl had dropped the paper on Linda's desk like yesterday's garbage and flounced out. She glared at Linda the whole term after that. A perpetual scowl. She wondered how she could have forgotten that girl. That D was a gift and the girl didn't know it.

She pushed the seat as far back as it would go which wasn't very far. On her second date with Jimmy—when his pickup was in the shop—they had tried to neck in her front seat. She had worked the side lever to the seat so that it went lower and lower. Jimmy was a bit shocked to find them almost level but for all her maneuvering, the steering wheel had dug into Jimmy's long, lanky frame like a black umbrella in the hand of some strict duenna and kept them apart. The back seat would have been slightly better but she didn't dare suggest that. And Jimmy wouldn't, not on the second date.

The car was a gift from her parents. They hadn't been pleased with her decision to chuck the Bronx and head to parts unknown. Unknown to them, at least. They lived the Steinberg New Yorker cover, all her New York friends did, where the map of the world petered out at 11th avenue, where Russia, Japan, China, and LA were mere dots on the consciousness of the mind. Kentucky didn't make it on that map, even as a dot. All her parents knew of Kentucky was the Derby, family feuds, and guns. Her father had heard that there were lots of guns in Kentucky. The Bronx wasn't exactly known for its safe streets, she told them, but it didn't make any difference. The Bronx they had lived with all their lives. Kentucky was a new concept.

Maybe if she'd been wearing her gun the evaluations would have been better. Her gun. Incredible. But everybody had nagged. A woman alone. Even Dr. Lowery. She had pushed the seat so far back, the gun poked its head out from under. She pushed it back. A lady's special, pearl handle, not too heavy but effective the salesman had told her. Lock it in the glove compartment, Jimmy told her, but what good would that do? She'd never find the key in time. Besides she didn't want to see it. She used her glove compartment. It was better out of sight. She didn't need it.

The secretaries had edited the worst comments, the comments they deemed improper or just plain mean. The pages were littered with short and long black lines as if wartime censors had edited the letters. It was like some kind of code she couldn't decipher. Linda hugged her breasts. She could imagine what they'd said. Nothing she hadn't heard a thousand times from construction workers back in New York. She was a lot less safe back there. What did her father know about being safe? If he had his way, she'd be in well-lighted places with plenty of people twenty-four hours a day. Her mother, too. But she was grown, twenty-six, and she couldn't live her life like that. She wouldn't. Her father would have taken Mrs. Nelson's side, wouldn't like her sitting alone in the back parking lot in the early morning, next to a wood. Would have taken from her this quiet time, the time she needed to get through the day. Bloody Harlan, he read to her. Bloody Breathitt. Half the eastern counties claimed the epithet.

But it wasn't like that. It was peaceful, as peaceful as a Southern Vermont. And the people gentle, no threat. Her father's worry couldn't be her worry. She had had to get away. She pressed her right hand on her forehead and grabbed the back of her neck with her left. She twisted. The tension popped out of her shoulders.

"Miz Eliot?" She leaped in her seat at the sound. A man was standing a couple feet from her open window. He must have come out of the woods but she hadn't heard him. She recognized the voice but couldn't make him out at first. Gradually his features came into focus. Oh, Hugh, she thought, Hugh Richie, ashamed of her momentary fright, one of her eight o'clock's. He was only a year or so younger than she was, 25, he had told her. He stood there—she wondered how long he'd been standing there—smiling. She straightened out her skirt which had pulled to mid-thigh while she was twisting her neck. Hugh didn't turn his head away while she was adjusting it. A nice show, she thought, more irritated than flustered.

Hugh's red hair poked out from under the mandatory cap. He was tall, as tall as Jimmy, but more muscled. He must have worked out, something Jimmy would never do. It smacked too much of vanity, though Jimmy did run. Hugh carried an old navy jacket draped over his shoulder. The sun was finally up, the mist almost gone. She noticed that the hints of green she had seen before were strands of plastic trash bags caught in the roots of the trees like tattered decorations. Red and blue Pepsi cans and yellow potato chip bags clumped together underneath the bushes. Some Vermont, she thought.

"Kind of far back to be parking, ain't it?" Hugh asked.

"I like the quiet," she answered, feeling like she'd been discovered doing something illicit. "And the walk is nice, too," she continued, unfolding herself from the Tercel. He stood there quietly, not bothering to conceal his stare.

"Well, I'll walk with you then if you don't mind," he smiled at her like he was asking for a date. For a giddy moment, she thought he might offer her his arm. But Eastern Kentucky boys didn't offer arms, even on dates. She turned a glint eye on him, but he kept smiling. He'd be good looking, she thought vaguely, if he wasn't her student.

"That would be fine," she answered, definitely not smiling, as she marched on ahead of him to the college.

Chapter 2

Sometimes she felt as if Kerry Campbell, her office mate, had been especially assigned as her guide to Appalachia. The assignment wasn't his idea, she knew, though she also knew he liked the view from his desk. The tension had returned to her neck. She began her twist.

"Holy shit! Just like that girl in *The Exorcist*. You upchuck green vomit, too?" he swiveled in his chair, a big man, going a bit paunchy at 32, his smile a white line of teeth between mustache and beard.

"Only on St. Patrick's day when I've been drinking green beer."

"Green beer. You sure are fancy up in New Yark, New Yark."

She had thought, at first, that his accent was real—and it was—but put on thick for the "foreigners," as if he'd been raised in Blackey, a coal town so isolated even most Peril residents hadn't been to it, instead of up on the "Hill" in Peril. As if he'd been educated by the relatives of the local politicians instead of an eastern prep school with a degree from Vandy. But he was a native, a Campbell, one of thousands of Campbells in the area. Related to everybody. Everybody was related to everybody. She'd learned not to comment on anyone after complaining about a secretary to the president only to discover that she was his second and third cousin. Kerry warned her.

"Don't be talking about nobody, Honey, until you check out which degree of cousin you're bad-mouthing. Anything beyond third cousin is OK. We call them kissing cousins. We marry our kissing cousins." He had married his. He had left the county a half dozen times, sometimes for years at a stretch. But he kept coming back.

"Why do you keep moving in and out?" she had asked him once.

"Now, honey, you mean to ask me why I keep moving in. Everybody knows why you move out. Slow learner, honey. I'm a

7

recidivist. They keep swinging the jail door both ways and I keep mistaking out for in."

"They give those fellows life after awhile, don't they?" She was on touchy ground. She always was with Kerry.

"Life in these here mountains? That'd be cruel and unusual punishment, wouldn't it, honey? They're OK to visit, kind of like they say about New Yark, but life? Don't you worry, honey, I'm gonna' break free one of these days. How long you visiting for, honey?"

There was the barb. "What makes you think I'm visiting?"

"You fixing to stay? Hoo, boy. You like us that much?"

Her first student conference of the day interrupted any more talk of green beer. Kerry, she knew, was irritated by her constant conferences, his desk was barely three feet away so they became his conferences, too, but she defended them. One on one she could make things clearer. Or at least, that was her theory.

She hated admitting it, but it was also useful having a male nearby. Kept the libidos under control. Not that she worried too much about that. She'd never been in a place where the males were more polite. In the Bronx, she had spent half her time fending off passes. But not one student had made a pass at her since she'd been in Kentucky. "Maybe they've heard about my gun," she joked to Jimmy. The boy, today, had slicked his hair back—she hoped not for her. He kept smiling and nodding his head as she talked but she didn't know if he was hearing, understanding. She tried to catch his eye. "My face is up here,' she told him, and he blushed so deeply for a moment she thought he was going to faint. Kerry choked on his coffee and went into a five minute coughing spree.

"Lord a mighty, give a body warning," he told her when the boy had hastily retreated. "You sure were unfriendly to that boy. Why didn't you smile some?"

"I was telling him he failed. Or was going to, if he didn't listen." She already regretted the face comment. Stupid. She didn't feel like smiling.

"You especially smile when you give bad news. That way they don't take it personally." Kerry was trying to hand dab the coffee stains from his shirt and not having much luck. She felt a bit gleeful at the sight. "You sure are unfriendly up North."

In New York, smiling was an invitation to get personal. She'd picked up men inadvertently smiling at a thought or a book she was reading on the subway. But in Kentucky, a smile was like buttoning a blouse for a woman. You weren't really dressed without one.

"When do you get to frown?"

"In your casket. It's considered bad taste to smile when you're dead. Of course, you're supposed to smile at a dead person. Try to cheer them up a bit. And you can frown if you've got a gun in your hands. You can do anything with a gun in your hands."

She was going to have to get the gun out from under the seat then. She looked at Kerry, gazed at him for a second, and she could see he was a bit taken back by her stare. "Guns and smiles, is that it?" He looked puzzled. She handed him her pile of evaluations. "Why don't they like me?'

He looked at her seriously and for a moment she thought he might actually tell her. The truth. But then his smile came back. "Why, honey, they like you. They have to like you after you come all the way from New Yark, New Yark just in order to educate them. Of course, sometimes you might aggravate folks some by giving out that you know a bit more than they do."

That comment was on half the evaluations. "She thinks she knows everything."

"I thought that was what I was paid to do, know more than they do."

Kerry's eyes widened the way they did whenever she fell into it completely. Talking with him was like playing winter soup poker, the game where a third of the cards were wild. Only she didn't know what the wild cards were.

"You are, honey, you are. A very big sum by local standards now that they're laying off at the mines again. But mostly you're paid to make us feel that what we don't know ain't worth knowing. Put a New Yark seal on our ignorance so to speak." He looked mournful as if she was a particularly slow student. But he was smiling. "We're mighty discouraging material for missionaries. Been that way for a hundred years."

9

"I'm no goddamn missionary."

Kerry laughed out loud at that. "Hooey. I guess you ain't with language like that. Excuse me, I keep forgetting. No jobs in New Yark?"

I came to make a difference, she wanted to tell him but knew what he'd do with a line like that. She looked out the window. That view was what she came for, too. The mountain by the side of the school had a thick growth of ash, maple, dogwood and red bud interspersed with pine. The spring would be beautiful, everybody told her. Her first Appalachian spring. But Kerry would pounce on that, too. He was especially alert when he smelled poetry in the air. She had pointed to the trees once and he had nodded. "Another 10, 15 years and we'll be ready to clear cut again, just in time for the coal giving out. Good times a coming."

She was still pondering the "know everything" comments.

"You lecture," he said.

"So does Tom Black. He booms his opinions everywhere." The walls were thin. She felt like she could teach Tom's history classes herself. He always got great evaluations.

"Why, honey, everybody knows what Tom's going to tell them. The secretaries know. He told their older brothers and sisters the same thing. Heck, he gave the same lecture to some of their parents. It's a great comfort to know what you're going to be told. You keep hitting a body with the unexpected. That's downright unsettling."

"You do, too."

"Oh, but, honey, I'm a good ol' boy. They mostly forgive my education on account of I came back down to my raisin' after just a little time of getting above it."

"You're no good ol' boy." She gathered up the graded essays for her eight o'clock. He wasn't going to tell her anything useful.

"Why, honey, sure I am. We're all good ol' boys around here. But you ain't." He slip-slid his eyes down her tailored suit, resting on her breasts. He pushed things. She made herself not blush. "Nobody's gonna' mistake you for a good ol' boy."

Chapter 3

"Describe somebody close to you. No mothers. Yes, OK, grand-mothers. Be sure to follow the format I handed out. But be original."
Hugh's essay hadn't followed the format.

I don't know that I can recall my first memory of Mamaw. She was just there—like the hollow we lived in which is named for her great granddaddy. Richie Creek. I don't know how many greats that makes for me. She was big, even back then, 'cause she loved to eat. That was one of the many reasons she never cared for Mamma. Mamma's a skinny gal who still watches her figure. When Daddy brought Mamma home the first time, he says Mamaw just looked at her and asked, "Where's the rest of her?"

"If you don't watch it, no one else will," Mamma says, talking about her figure, and just picks at her food like it's been hanging in the smokehouse just one day too long.

"You gonna' eat those vittles or what?" Mamaw says, it gets on her nerves so. "There's plenty other creatures who'll eat them if you don't," she says and ends up grabbing the plate and tossing the food out the door to the pigs or the dogs—whoever gets there first.

When I was little I knew Mamaw could lick anybody in the hollow. Nobody dared tackle her except Papaw once when he was almost dead drunk from some home made. She just backhanded him out the door and he staggered off to the barn where he spent the next three nights. She made sure he didn't freeze to death, but that was about all. Mamaw never did like drinking and she liked it even less after that. So did Papaw.

I come to live with her when I was about nine, I guess. I mean full time. Before that I ate maybe half my meals there—simple kind of meals. Mamaw likes to eat, but she don't believe in wasting too much time on the cooking. Too much to do to spend your days stirring a pot or watching some fatback fry. It will fry whether you watch it or not. If it got a bit signed, well, hell——or heck—Mamaw don't believe in cussing—it all went into the same stomach. If you didn't want it, there were plenty of other creatures who did.

I was one of the creatures who did. I never complained. It seemed good enough to me, especially after Daddy forgot to come back from Louisville or Cincinnati or Chicago——or wherever he ended up, and Mamma found two, three others to help her keep watch on her figure. It was a nice figure. It still is. But I think I like Mamaw's better. Just from my point of view. It fills up the whole doorway just like her food fills up the whole plate. Good and plain. It does the job.

Chapter 4

She hadn't noticed anything different about Hugh at first. He was a little older than most of the students, coming from a stint in the navy, but she had a sprinkling of older students. He slouched down in his chair the same way all the males did, hid half his face behind the same caps they all wore. Some of the young women had the good student posture, sitting up straight, nodding and smiling at the points she made—even when, as she discovered when she called on them, they hadn't a clue as to what she was talking about. Looking interested wasn't a masculine thing to do, she gathered—at least not in English class.

Hugh was interested, though, or at least he paid attention. She'd question him and other males occasionally. He was always with her, sometimes ahead of her. But it was his writing that really surprised her. She hadn't expected the originality. It was crude writing, she'd work on that, but something was there. It was more than she could find in any of her other students.

And he actually talked in class. She couldn't even get the young women, good students, to speak beyond a line or two. But Hugh would talk, would argue even.

"You sure about that, ma'am?" He almost grinned when he challenged her. She remembered Kerry's line. She shouldn't take it personal. She'd been linking the rising homicide rate to handgun ownership statistics.

"It makes sense, doesn't it?"

"Don't know about that, ma'am. Seems like we've always owned guns around here. But lately, we've been shooting each other more.

Twelve dead and barely holding. Pretty high for a little county like us. And the year ain't half over."

He sat in the front row——the other males competed for the back row. He stretched his long legs out in front of him. She had almost tripped over him more than once—pirouetting over his feet. He'd pull them back in for a while but gradually they'd inch back out.

"Many factors might go into a homicide rate. But it's so much easier to kill somebody with a gun than with a knife or with your bare hands. You have to come close. If you wanted to kill me, in a rage perhaps, you couldn't from across the room." She had moved to the back of the room, closer to the fellows in the end row. They closed their legs like Catholic schoolgirls at her approach. She made the class turn in their chairs to follow her. They looked at the distance she had put between herself and Hugh. She felt a bit flustered, irritated at herself for coming up with such a personal analogy. Hugh paused, as if he was appraising the distance, too.

"I don't want to kill you ma'am. Close or far."

The class released its tension in a loud laugh. She let herself laugh, too. "I'm glad," she said. "I don't want to kill you, either. Or anybody," she added, thinking of the gun underneath her front seat. She felt a bit hypocritical. She marched to the front of the room, grabbed some chalk and started writing. "And you're right. It'd be interesting to see what other factor lead to homicide. Maybe right here in Peril County." She began to get excited. It'd be a wonderful research project. It was so hard to make research projects real to students, especially freshmen." She wrote: WHY DO PEOPLE GET KILLED IN PERIL COUNTY in large letters on the board. She turned, expectantly.

The silence that greeted her wasn't the usual kind—a mixture of shyness and diffidence. She had their attention, but they were looking at her with something that appeared to be shock, as if they couldn't believe what she was saying. What now? she thought. For a moment, she didn't know what to do. They were pulling back. She looked to the few students she had learned to count on when things got stuck, but even their faces were shut down. Only Hugh looked interested, curious, but not ready to volunteer. No matter. She called on him as her best chance.

Hugh pushed his hat back and paused a moment before he answered. She thought for a second he was going to pass, but he grinned and decided to come to her rescue. "No need for any research project, ma'am, to figure out why folks get shot in Peril County. Anybody could tell you." And now she felt the class turning its look on him, as if he was breaking ranks somehow, about to spill some secrets to the foreigner. "Do your drinking in the wrong bars. Get born into the wrong families. You do either and the odds of getting shot go up a whole lot. Do your drinking at home, be born right and you'll liable to live to a long old age, even in Perry."

Nobody chuckled. She stifled her own laugh into a cough. Two young men tensed up like they were ready to leap from their chairs. She walked towards them, not knowing what she was going to do. They sat back in their chairs as she approached. She stood there in front of them, hoping to calm them, but they began to squirm more at her nearness. Somebody started shouting in the front of the classroom.

"You think everybody who's killed is born in the wrong family? Or went drinking in some trashy bar." Amy, a quiet girl who Linda had never heard speak above a mumble was out of her seat, face flushed. She still wore braids as if she were twelve instead of eighteen. The brains were swinging behind her like two whips.

Hugh's seat was only one away from Amy's. He turned to her when she started shouting with that casual look some men put on before a fight, as if to say the prospect didn't worry them at all. He paused while she stood there and Linda thought he might not say anything. She willed him to be quiet. "Amy," she started, but so quietly nobody heard her. Amy continued yelling.

"You Richies must know all about trashy families and bars."

She saw Hugh tense up but he continued smiling. "Maybe so. I guess a whole bunch of us know about trashy families."

"Hugh," Linda said, louder, but still no one heard her. Hugh had sat up straighter in his desk, as if it wasn't polite to slouch when someone was shouting at you.

"Of course, you don't always have to be born into a trashy family to get shot," he continued. "Sometimes a body just blows away the good fortune they were born with and ups and marries into a no account one. You end up getting shot that way, too."

Somehow Amy and Hugh had closed the small distance between them. Linda felt a little giddy. No need for a gun in that space. It's time to end this, she thought, and she started to move quickly towards the board. But Amy was in Hugh's face before she reached it. Her sister wasn't trash, Amy was yelling, her sister hadn't married trash. She screamed and hit at Hugh who parried her blows easily but didn't hit back. He had stopped smiling at least, Linda saw. He looked sad, almost regretful. Amy's friend, Sherry, had jumped up and was yelling, too. She stood behind Amy, trying to grab her arms. Everyone in the class were on their feet, the two girls nearest Hugh scrambling to get out of the way, the boys in the back row hooting encouragement. Linda couldn't move.

"What's going on here!" Tom Black's booming voice made everybody jump and quiet down. Sherry was able finally to pull Amy away. Tom had been teaching next door. He looked over at Linda, disappointment and disapproval in his eyes.

"A discussion," she finally managed to say, "about gun control. It got out of hand."

He continued staring at her as if she wasn't making any sense. She wasn't making any sense. "Gun control? Maybe a discussion on class control would serve you better." He turned and left.

Amy had returned to her seat, her face in her hands, Sherry next to her, murmuring something. Linda looked at Hugh. He was pale and glum looking, not pretending to be unaffected. She put the chalk back down with a clack that made half the class jump. They had forgotten about her. She understood the look they gave her now. Don't talk about it. Leave it alone. She breathed deeply.

"Sometimes," she started quietly, "local topics are difficult," she paused, they hung on her words like they had never done before, "to research. Not enough resources. Other subjects might work better." She could feel rather than hear them let out a collective breath. "Like Vietnam," and a peaceful glaze began to descend back over their eyes. Vietnam. It could have been World War I. A nice peaceful war. English class again as they knew it. Hugh leaned back and flipped his baseball

16

cap down over his eyes. Amy kept her head down, Sherry kept murmuring. Back to almost normal.

If Amy had had a gun, Linda thought, but didn't want to finish the image. What had happened, she wondered, what had she stumbled on? She kept Amy and Hugh in her sight. For the first time, she realized how apart Hugh seemed from the rest of the class. He was one of them. But somehow wasn't.

Research Paper Idea: Sketch One:

I thought I'd explore killings in Peril County. After that ruckus in class, it might be exciting. Only I think I'll steer clear of Amy's sister. Might be better, don't you think?

One of my cousins, I got cousins everywhere, works down at the courthouse and she let me see two cases. Just two fights. Nothing to them really. A black guy in a bar killing a white guy—that fight just erupted. Second degree manslaughter. The other a stabbing in Jerry's parking lot—first degree man-slaughter. I guess because they came ready to tangle—with knives.

Maybe I should change topics to justice in Peril County because the black kid with the second degree conviction got ten years and the white kid with first degree was told to move his tail down to Florida with probation.

You'd be pleased as an English teacher to know that it was well-written epistles that made all the difference. The white kid's file is full of these real nice letters from real nice folks. I'll show them to you but my cousin might have to skedadle to Florida herself if it gets out so we got to keep it private. But they were good letters—and from good people: the chief of police, the superintendent of schools, and the topper, the prosecutor. He was real sorry to have to prosecute a boy from such a nice family. The Judge just had to take that into account. And that boy learned his lesson. Some people might think having to live in Florida for a few years ain't that hard, but around here we call it cruel and unusual punishment. I'm

17

surprised his lawyer—you see that name, he's maybe the most famous lawyer in the state, starts at fifty thousand a shot I hear—let the judge exile him there. The least he could have gotten the boy was Louisville, especially at his prices.

The black kid's file only has three letters—his mamma's, a friend's, and his own. Pretty sorry. What do you expect when you got a public defender for a lawyer? I know Amy thinks I called the family her sister married into trash but I sure didn't mean to. Her sister's husband got a real good lawyer, top money. You couldn't have been killed by a finer family.

So when you think about it, it's that black boy's own doing that he got ten years. He should have been saving for a real lawyer all these years. Or his family should have. Any fool could have told them he'd be bound to need one.

Chapter 5

Write about your town. That had stirred them. "I'm from Vicco," one boy protested. "Ain't no town to write about."

"There's always something," she persisted. "Just look harder."

"You can look all day and night," the boy continued. "There ain't no town to write about."

"Well then write about the town that used to be there," she said, and the boy had slumped into his chair in despair.

Hugh had written about Peril.

I guess Peril's my town though Mamaw don't think we belong to any town. But Richies been there almost as long as the Cornets. Of course I got Cornet cousins by the dozens. That ain't saying much. Everybody got Cornet cousins. Except you. And I don't know, you might even. They got the first Cornet standing in front of the court building, with pigeons draped all over him. Only fair considering he probably shot two million carrier pigeons in his lifetime. I figure those town cousins are just getting some of their own back on old Cornet.

He had thirteen sons and as many daughters. And they all had about the same. So you might be related to him.

Peril used to be what my idea of a town looked like—till I went off to the navy and visited some real places. Now the main street downtown kind of reminds me of a movie set built for an old-time Western. They got all these impressive three story fronts, but if you skirt around on back there ain't but one little puny story to their rears. Mamaw says that's what city folks are like—all up front with nothing behind them. Mamaw's real tough on town folks—maybe because we're related to half of them. Or maybe she just don't want me to become one of them. Like Daddy. Like Mamma. I tell her, Mamaw, the town's good for some things but that just makes her mad. Of course, she says, the town's good for some things. She never said it wasn't. But it's bad for a whole lot of other things.

Mamaw mostly has the bars in mind. We're about the only town in the mountains you can get a drink so we got a few. I don't bother telling her that most of the bars ain't too bad. I might as well preach that there's devils and then there's devils. And some of those bars are basic training in rough. A navy buddy of mine came to visit me and thought he'd have a peaceful beer in a nice small town tavern while he waited for me to finish school. I'm just glad he made it out of that saloon alive.

Of course, you want to hear about the feuds being from up North. Feuding always just sounded like regular old killing to me and we got enough of that still, but the feuding most folks talk about makes it sounds romantic like, like the killing was special. I guess the folks involved think maybe all killings are special. I guess that girl Amy does. Those feud killings are way before my time, or even Mamaw's. French and Eversole families, shot 12 men in one day back in 1888. I asked Mamaw if we were related to them. She said she reckoned we were though she didn't know how exactly. But if there's trouble, she said, there's a Richie in the thick of it. How come you married a Richie, then, I asked, you being a Richie and knowing their propensity for trouble? She and Papaw are third cousins. She looked suspicious at that word "propensity" like I was trying to put something over on her, but mostly she just looked wore out like it was one silly question too many. "Had to marry somebody," she told me.

People usually think the name of the town has something to do with danger when really it got it from some naval hero back in the war of 1812. Pretty silly for a mountain town. Maybe they thought the poor old Kentucky river would make a kind of seaport though nothing much bigger than a barge floats in it—and a few houses when it floods. And lots of trash. Trash of all kinds. But we fit the name eventually—just like Mamaw says. You grow into a name.

"I grow into my name yet, Mamaw?"

"You might grow into a name you don't want," she warns. Like my daddy or my mamma, she might add only she's too polite. Or me. "You ain't got your good name, yet," she'd concede, " but you got time."

Peril's earned its name though it ain't nearly so dangerous as some people think. It's just full of perils. Keep your eyes open, Mamaw says. No need to fall into the holes. People dig their own holes, she says.

"All of them?" I ask..

"You just keep your eyes open," she keeps saying. "You'll be fine."

One big peril is that folks take things personal around here. You might have found that out. They think you're talking about them when really you're just making a point. Like that girl Amy thinking I was talking about her family being trashy. That's why we're so polite most of the time, even Mamaw in her own way.

Once in a while, you think the hell with it. I'm gonna' say what I feel like. But mostly that's a mistake.

Sometimes you can't avoid the perils no matter how polite you are or how wide your eyes are open. Even that muddy old river makes it way through town every seven years or so like it graduated to ocean over night. "Folks building on a flood plain ought to expect to be flooded," Mamaw says every time it happens—which don't mean she ain't down there doing everything she can to help. But she knows folks got to build somewhere, got to marry somebody. And our own little creek has imagined itself a river more than once. The nice folks, the good families like that prosecutor was talking about know better to build too close to water. They build up high, up on the mountain—like Mr. Campbell's family.

You might notice how we divide people into categories around here. Mostly nice people and the rest. I always wanted to hear Mamaw on the subject but I know what she'd say. That there ain't no respectable people. Each person's got to earn that name all by hisself. Then she'd kind of look at me hard like the jury hadn't come back with its decision about me yet. I'd have to tell her she was wrong. The verdict's been in for some time.

I don't know much what else to tell about Peril. It's mostly about coal or selling things to people who dug the coal. Like alcohol—the coal mine owners didn't want drinking around the mines. Except it's survived—not like most of the coal towns around here. I don't know what that poor ol' boy's going to say about Vicco. Or Blackie. Or Bulan. I don't think there's more than twenty people left in Bulan and it used to be a fair size place. Those coal towns are mostly gone now. Like the carrier pigeons. Or ghost towns. I bet we got more ghost towns around here than any place out West. Even Peril ain't got but five thousand people or so. Year round. Of course, last fall with the Black Gold days, you'd of thought we had graduated up to Lexington, or even Louisville. They came into town to see some silly TV stars that used our name for their show. Don't matter that the show is set in Georgia or that they added an extra r to the name, or that as far as anybody can tell, the show don't have a damn thing to do with anything around here. They were honored. That's the saddest thing. They were honored.

I guess they came to see Walin Jennings, too. Did you hear how he wouldn't go on till ol' Vern Cooper opened the bank vault on Saturday night and paid him off in cash? Wouldn't take a check. Then he only sang an hour or so. Old Walin wasn't going to have anything put over on him. He'd heard of places like Peril. He had his eyes wide open and wasn't about to fall in no hole.

Hell, most people know all about places like Peril. You ask anybody up North or out West. Or even Lexington and Louisville. They'll tell you all about Peril and the people who live there. Doesn't much matter if they've been here or not. Somehow they know. Their verdict's in, too.

She called Hugh in for a conference. He was late. Kerry had already left. He didn't stay around for her "conferencing" if he could help it. She'd been staring at the trees on the hillside, watching their spindly fingers stretch their shadows until they were half way across the parking lot. Second growth, she thought, remembering Kerry's line. Each branch tip was rounded into buds—-waiting to bloom. Soon. What did it matter? Second growth. Third growth.

"Miz Eliot?" He had startled her again. He closed the door behind her. Keep it open, she started to say but let it go. He pulled a chair up by the side of her desk so she had to turn to face him. He looked at her expectantly. He pushed his cap back so he could see her better. No man ever removed a cap as far as she knew.

"You're late," she said, but he just nodded like she'd been telling him some news that didn't have much to do with him. He waited quietly while she fussed about in her briefcase, looking for his paper. She wished now she had told him to keep the door open, but it was too late to say it now.

"SPELLING! FORMAT!" were blazoned across the front page of his essays. In red. She paused.

"Is Mamaw still alive?" she heard herself asking.

He grinned and stretched his long legs out in front of him.

"Going strong," he said. "Getting everybody else going strong, too. She don't think a job and school's enough for me to do. I think the only thing that scares Mamaw are a pair of idle hands. Devil's workshop. Has me working night and day on the homestead. This here conference is about the only break I've got all week."

Mamaw. Linda leaned towards Hugh, eager to find out more about Mamaw. "Homestead? Do you live on a farm?"

"Farm's a fancy name for it." He pulled his chair a little closer to explain. "It's mostly hill with just a few places Mamaw calls flat but

23

nobody else would. Of course, they're flattening out all around us." Hugh's face tensed, but he was smiling. "They got one of them thirty million dollar strip machines gouging out the other side of the hollow. Mamaw and me gonna' be left stranded one day, the only hill left, like one of those mesas they got out in New Mexico." Linda had pulled her chair back as Hugh explained. He hadn't moved closer.

Strip mining. Jimmy told her it was ruining the country. He had gotten her involved with the Fair Tax people. "Do-gooders" Kerry called them. Most of them outsiders like Jimmy. A few natives.

"You don't own the mineral rights?" She felt some of Jimmy's indignation. She began to picture Mamaw stranded.

"Depends on who's deciding." He didn't look mad, himself. "Mamaw never sold her mineral rights. Neither did her daddy or his daddy. But Uncle Freddy sold off his back in the forties."

"Why should that affect you or Mamaw, one way or the other?" Linda had almost forgotten the essay. She covered up the words SPELLING! FORMAT! with her notebook, embarrassed somehow by them.

"Well, ma'am," he began, and he sounded like Kerry all of a sudden, trying to explain some local complexity to her—but not really expecting her to understand. Even his accent reminded her of Kerry, though Hugh's was a subtler lighter version. "Title deeds are kind of a cottage industry around here. Lawyers been making their living interpreting them for almost two hundred years, I figure. Some have got real good at it. Especially coal lawyers. But don't you worry, we're working on it. Besides, those machines ain't all bad. They sure do open up the view. Almost got a river view now and we never did before. I told Mamaw we should put up a sign and rent rooms. In between, it does looks like some kind of moonscape, but that don't much matter. You get used to it. And the sun creeps in half an hour earlier without the mountain to climb over. I told Mamaw that should make her happy. Get to working earlier. Get me working earlier."

She shook her head, ignoring his humor. "Can't you stop them?"

"Stop them? It's progress, ma'am. And jobs, too. Besides, what they got from Uncle Freddy, they paid for. We're just trying to keep them off Mamaw's land. Especially the graveyard. We don't think he sold the graveyard land. Didn't own it. Problem is, nobody's clear who does own it. He's using it now, though."

"Who?"

"Uncle Freddy. I just hope one of those machines don't dig him up with the coal."

"He couldn't have known what he was doing." The broad form deeds were the chief target of the fair tax people. She felt indignant. She looked at Hugh whose smile had finally faded.

"Too dumb, huh?"

"Not dumb. They just didn't have machines like that in the forties. He couldn't have known."

"I guess not." Hugh pulled his legs in and sat up straighter. "But I sell the coal on the land, I might think the people buying will find some way of getting that coal. Unless they're mighty stupid people paying for what they can't use. You think Uncle Freddy thought those coal people were dumb as stone? Maybe he thought he was putting something over on them. Won't he be surprised when they dig him up?"

She had somehow offended the tender Appalachian sensibility. She didn't know how. She pulled the notebook off the essay and took a breath. He spotted the words and grinned again.

"I've read your latest," she began. "You can't keep getting A's with spelling like this," she said.

"That mean I'm getting A's?" he asked.

"When you've corrected them. And follow the format," she added, though she didn't really want him to anymore. She liked the way he meandered about though it wasn't what she had had in mind when she assigned the topics. For a second she couldn't think of anything else to say to him.

"Why don't you write about it? Strip mining. Uncle Freddy. The cemetery. It could be your research project."

Hugh looked dubious. "Sounds kind of heavy. The whole Richie saga. Maybe too much for this ol' boy."

She was too tired for good ol' boy routine. "You're too damn smart to think you're anything but damn smart so knock off the good ol' boy routine."

He perked up at the damn. It still qualified as cussing in Peril. A lady English teacher cussing took on even more interest. "Well, I'll give it a try, ma'am," stretching his legs out again and inching his seat closer one more time. She stood up so quickly he almost tipped over.

"Good," she said, grabbing her coat and heading for the door before she remembered his essay. "And correct that spelling."

"Yes, ma'am," he answered, taking hold of his paper before she let go so that for a second they formed a kind of bridge. "Anything to make the grade, Miz Eliot."

Chapter 6

"Damn it!" She skidded away from the ditch, missing it by inches. The coal truck was almost on top of her, blaring its horn like a train. She hadn't realized it was going that fast and was scrambling out of its lane. "Stupid bitch," the driver shouted as he shot past. The coal was heaped in the back like a small black pyramid, small pebbles of it hitting her windshield. "You're supposed to have a tarp," she yelled back but he was already a speck on the highway. She was on her second windshield.

"Wouldn't be a road without coal trucks," Kerry told her when she complained. "Way they see it, you're intruding on their space. Mighty kind of them to let you pass."

Mighty kind. Narrow twisty lanes and roads so shaded by the mountains the ice patches wouldn't melt until April. If then. She had arrived in deep summer the year before, when the narrow valleys were so crowded in green that the roads snaked like rivers through the Amazon rain forest. The Kudzu vines were like giant boa constrictors, entangling everything, even the telephone poles. How wonderful, she thought, till Jimmy had explained that they killed everything. Like Marvel's line. "Annihilating all that's made to a green thought in a green shade." Annihilating. Covering everything.

But not in March. The Kudzu hung in brown frizzy strands, limp and dirty. The ditch she had just missed was filled with trash.

Her rented house was up a settled hollow about three miles from the college, an A-frame built quick to catch the tourists in the boom seventies. Only the tourists had never come and the boom had passed. And the house had begun to tilt—they hadn't let the land settle long enough. Linda liked the tilt. A house with an attitude. The rent was cheap.

Everybody gave her grief when she rented it——a woman alone up a hollow. She had bought the gun to settle them down. Thank God, her parents didn't know a hollow from a Hilton. "They raped the chemistry teacher's wife," Mrs. Nelson whispered to her, bringing her an extra bookcase she had scared up from storage. She felt sorry for the young woman teacher, so far from her family.

"But she didn't live alone," Linda answered, wondering where she was going to fit the bookcase without taking more of Kerry's space. She seemed to pick up parents everywhere. "Safer than the Bronx," she added and Mrs. Nelson couldn't argue with that. Besides the hollow had only one way in and one way out and her landlords lived at the bottom of the road, keeping an eye on their investment. They would protect her. She was the only one who had answered their ad.

She parked her car by her landlord's driveway. It was a half-mile hike almost straight up to her house but she wasn't driving till the ice melted. To make it to the top, she'd needed to roar the engine, foot pressed down all the way. She'd prayed not to meet anyone coming the other way. She'd lost her nerve her last try and had been stuck on a curve right next to an edge that looked more cliff than ditch. Afraid to move. Up or down. She was wondering desperately whether she should just jump free, let the car roll off by itself, when she spotted one of her landlord's boys, a tall, skinny fourteen-year-old. He smiled when he saw her, he was one of her only regular visitors. He looked puzzled when he saw she had the door open and her left leg out on the road, pushing against it like a brake.

"I'm stuck," she said, and he looked more puzzled as if she meant that she was stuck in the car. "I can't go up or down."

He slid into the passenger side when he understood, easing his foot onto the brake pedal while she hopped out to safety.

"You want to go up or down?" he asked, as if there were a choice.

"Down," she shuddered, vowing never again till Spring. "Wait!" she shouted before he started, and she bent down between his legs, fumbling for something. For a second he looked as scared as she'd been until she pulled the gun out from under the seat.

"Oh," he nodded, as if people pulled guns from between his legs all the time. He spun the Tercel around like it was a jeep, barely turning to see where the road ended and the ravine began. "Just leave the keys under the seat," she shouted and he waved.

Most of her neighbors kept to themselves, waving when she passed. She had visited most of them, thinking that was the thing to do, and they had been friendly. But they hadn't visited back. The only neighbors she really knew were Caroline and Sister, two older ladies who lived right above her landlords, fellow outsiders though they'd been there over thirty years. Sister was a double outsider, a Catholic nun in a land of Baptists. Caroline was a nurse-midwife in Hyden. She'd actually drop by unannounced—she and the landlord's boy the only neighbors who did.

She bent over to change her shoes for the climb. She wrinkled her nose. Real clodhoppers. She reached under the seat and shoved the gun into her briefcase. Ladies' special or not, it added to the weight of the briefcase, already stuffed with papers and texts. The road faced north. Large patches of iced skimmed its surface. She skated flat across them. The hill across from her had southern exposure. It was like a different season over there, she thought. Water ran down it in steady driblets. She could see sprouts of greens. Not trash bags, she thought. The wispy, delicate green of new leaves. The buds on the Tulip trees were half open and there were spots of lavender she imagined must be clumps of violets, like dabs of color on an Impressionist painting. She sighed. The future, she thought. Hang on.

She pushed forward, upward, feeling the climb in her thighs. She rounded the last bend. The final stretch was the worst, almost straight up. The backpack straps dug into her shoulders. She paused for breath. She looked into the woods—dark, as if the sun wasn't still high in the sky. Lonely, as if there weren't houses hidden behind almost every turn. "Oh," she said. She had spotted a purple patch about forty yards in, a splash so vivid against the brown grass it almost looked as if someone had spilled paint on the ground. A ray of bright sunlight had somehow angled itself in. The flowers stood next to a house as brown as the grass, a shack really. She thought maybe it was abandoned. She plunged off the road, needing to get closer. She knelt to smell them, slipping her backpack off, reaching out to touch the petals as gently as if they'd been a newborn's cheeks. She inhaled deeply. She needed this.

"Who are you?"

Linda looked up quickly. A woman about sixty was standing in the open doorway, holding a gun with a barrel so long it tipped to the ground out of weight, if not politeness. She wore a summer house dress that bared fleshy arms. She looked more muscled than heavy. The dress was a green print with faded white daisies. Linda had never seen her before. "Who are you?" the woman repeated.

"I'm your neighbor," Linda said, and was surprised to hear how calm she sounded. The woman wasn't actually pointing the gun at her, she was just holding it to let it know it was there. "I live at the top of the hill." Her backpack lay open in front of her. She could see her gun. It seemed like a toy next to the woman's.

"School teacher," the woman nodded, taking her in. Placing her. What must she look like, she thought, lavender suit and clodhoppers. "What you doing here?"

"I saw these beautiful violets," Linda started to explain, but stopped. The reason seemed silly, not good enough to trespass. "I wanted to take a closer look," she finished softly.

"Don't like folks poking around," the woman responded. "You best get on back." She lowered the gun farther, but she didn't smile. You don't need to smile with a gun in your hand, Linda remembered. She stood blocking the doorway though Linda could see a baby sleeping on the couch.

Linda nodded. "Sorry," she said and reached for her backpack. It tumbled and one of her high-heeled shoes spilled out. The woman looked curious. Linda shoved it back in and snapped the straps quickly. She'd have to tell Hugh. He was right. Danger everywhere, even sniffing flowers.

Jimmy was waiting for her, his pickup boldly parked next to the gully that bordered her driveway, one of his tires halfway over the edge. No room for error.

"Still walking?" he greeted her. He looked full of energy. It almost made her feel more tired than she was.

She pointed to his tires. "You'd walk if you had any sense. Though walking is getting dangerous, too."

"What do you mean?" he asked, but she just shook her head. "You know," he continued, "the mud is worse than the ice. Your road is just going to dissolve in the rain. You better get together with your neighbors and pour on a few loads of gravel."

"Not feeling too neighborly at present," she said. "What are you doing here in the middle of the day?" Jimmy worked long hours. She didn't usually see him till long after dark.

"We got a schedule?" He smiled at her, and she thought it must be his first smile of the day, a smile of pure happiness. He was glad to see her. She sat on the edge of the deck and he sat by her. She started to take off her clodhoppers but he finished the job for her. He pulled the shoes from her feet and started to rub her toes, the surest way to her heart he knew. Linda leaned back against the rail. The pressure of his fingers on her toes traveled like a warm line up her thighs.

"I want a bath," she said.

"I'll run one for you," he answered and his eagerness made her giggle. She looked at him critically. He wasn't handsome though he had a rough good looks. Too awkward. A big head on a skinny neck. He could hardly find a cap big enough. His hair stuck out from beneath like Zeppo Marx. He had beautiful eyes, but his nose was too big, crooked. Too many fights, too many demonstrations.

She felt his hands travel up to her ankles. His hands were a surprise, his fingers long and tapered like a pianist's. She found it hard to imagine them balled into fists, but she knew they had been. Years as a lawyer organizing the poor in the roughest North Philly neighborhoods. He'd still be there but Reagan had cut the funding.

"Ronny cut it himself?" she'd teased him.

"Himself," Jimmy had answered, as if Reagan had wielded the scissors personally. Politics were personal to Jimmy. From Philly to Peril. The Federal government still paid most of the bills for all Reagan's efforts. And he was happier than he'd been in Philly. Much happier.

"God moves in mysterious ways," he said, trying to sound ironic, but sounding serious instead. "I belong here."

"God a racist?" she asked. "He like Appalachian poor better than Philly poor?"

He laughed. All her teasing made him laugh. "I just do more good here." Racism had been the enemy in Philly. King Coal was the enemy here. A white boy had more luck fighting coal.

"I'll run my own bath," she told him, trying to move but not making it. His fingers felt so good. "You might think of a cold shower."

"Cold shower sounds good," he whispered. "Skip the bath. We'll take one together." His long fingers had returned to her toes, separately them one by one. She closed her eyes. "I hate this woman." The old lady's gun, pointed right at her. Coal trucks and ditches rose up to greet her. She opened them again.

"I want to show you something afterwards," Jimmy said, and she looked at him warily. What now? "Coal companies blasting people out of their homes. Right in your neighborhood."

"Oh, Jimmy," she said. "I'm so tired." She started to pull herself up again, but he put his hand on her shoulder.

"I know you are. But it won't take twenty minutes. And we'll rest first."

"Rest?" she laughed. "Is that what we're calling it?"

"Well," Jimmy smiled at her again, and she did feel rested. "We'll rejuvenate," and he laid his head on her ample breasts and nuzzled gently. He had switched his cap backwards, planning ahead she realized. She pulled it off and sailed it into the yard. His hair sprung up, liberated. He pressed his thighs against hers. She could feel the bulge in his jeans, wanting its own liberation. She reached out and traced the outline of his penis, softly, tenderly. He sucked in his breath as if it were the first time she had touched him. Every time she touched him, the newness of the experience amazed him. She pulled away quickly and finally made it to her feet. They were going to make it to the bed this time.

"So let's go rejuvenate," she said, and led him into the house.

Chapter 7

The house, or what was left of it, was at the edge of what could have been a battlefield. The land had been peeled away to a dark gray-black bone, as if it were an old grapefruit rind discarded after the coal-fruit of the earth was taken. Bushes and trees were tumbled up together on the edges of the field, their thin branches spiny fingers sticking through the earth, like victims of a massacre hastily buried by their killers. A slag heap was smoldering on one side of the field. A soft, spring breeze blew in their direction. The sulfur smell was overwhelming.

"Oh, God," Linda gasped. "It's an inferno." Jimmy had parked his pickup by the edge of the field. He hadn't said anything since he had turned off the engine. He nodded at her words. He kept his eyes on the field.

"Look at that." He pointed to the house. Linda hadn't even noticed the house. It looked more like a collapsed barn than a house, like one of hundreds that littered upstate New York. Jimmy leaped out of the pickup and headed towards it. Linda scrambled after him.

They paused at the front porch, or what was left of it. "This is a house?" She could smell, even through the sulfur, the soft rotten odor of old wet wood. Everything had the crumbly look of long decay.

"It used to be before the blasting knocked half of it down."

"Looks like it might have fallen down on its own eventually." She felt Jimmy stiffen at her words.

"Eventually's not now," Jimmy replied, turning his angry look from the house to her. She had used the coal company's argument.

Up close, Linda could see the faded painted shutters and an old flowerbed still pushing up crocuses. They picked their way around what had been the front parlor. It hadn't been as totally defeated as she first thought. But like an old woman who seems to be doing fine till a fall puts her under, the blasting had collapsed the house to one side as if its hip had snapped. Massive cracks split its foundations. Circling the house to the kitchen, the sink and old stove just visible, she saw the collapse was almost complete with parts of the ceiling joining the floor. Glass from the windows lay all about them.

"Mind that glass there!" A man's voice shouted a warning at her.

Linda let out a small shriek of surprise. A man and a woman looking like they were in their late sixties were hoeing a garden. The back of the house was a different world from the front. A large cultivated field ended in a grove of beaches and fir trees. The garden was less than a yard from the collapsed house. It started flat but climbed steeply within a few feet, so steeply Linda didn't know how the old folks kept their balance.

"Sorry," the old man nodded, leaning on his hoe. "Didn't meant to scare you none, but that glass is wicked sharp. Just getting our kitchen garden ready." He smiled. "Of course we ain't got no kitchen anymore." He was a small, skinny man. He looked cheerful, like he welcomed the interruption. The woman by him had paused a moment on seeing them. She was taller than he, with the stringy muscled arms of a countrywoman. She kept on hoeing, swinging the hoe like a pickaxe. Shards of dirt flew in her wake like the spray from a speedboat.

"Welcome to our homestead, Mr. O'Connell," the man continued. "Taking more photos?"

"Got enough photos," Jimmy replied. "Just wanted to show my friend the coal company's handiwork." He introduced Linda.

"The schoolteacher from New York." The old man wiped his hand on his britches before shaking Linda's outstretched one. Sometimes Linda felt like the whole county knew who she was. She felt awkward towering over the old man, but he looked contented staring up at her.

"Pull up a stump," he offered, as if it were the best chair in the house. "Mamma," he shouted for she had continued up the hill, "where's the cup for the water?"

"By the stump," the woman answered, not pausing in her swinging.

The man looked a little embarrassed at his wife's rudeness. "We're late planting," he explained, "what with all the excitement. Should have had the peas in a couple of weeks ago. The lettuce, too." He knelt on his haunches as if he wanted to stay lower than Linda." Don't seem much of a courting choice, him making you come out to this wreck."

"Jimmy's a different kind of courter," she said and the old man laughed.

Jimmy ignored the teasing. "It's a wreck now. But it was a beautiful house before."

The man looked a little doubtful. "Beautiful might be stretching it some. Needed a lot of work—more work than I was up to. Mamma could tell you about that. But it was ours. Had a few years left in it. Just like us."

Linda sipped the water the old man had poured for her. She spit it on the ground. The sulfur taste choked her like bad meat. Jimmy looked horrified, but the old man just laughed.

"I forgot to tell you about the sulfur. We're gotten so used to it we don't taste it no more. I wish I had something else to offer you to wash the taste away."

It was OK, Linda told him. Jimmy took the cup from her and drank the remaining water without flinching.

The man turned to Jimmy. "Mr. O'Connell, Mamma and me's been talking. Maybe we should take that offer."

Jimmy put down the cup. "Five thousand dollars? That's not an offer. It's an insult."

"It ain't much," the man agreed. "Wouldn't even pay for the lumber I'd need to rebuild. But it's hard to win with these coal outfits. The big ones fight you forever and the little ones just skip out."

"We got one right in the middle. Too little to fight forever. Too big to run away."

The man stretched to his feet, using his hoe like a cane. He looked unconvinced. "Five thousand's something at least." He continued looking at Jimmy, searching his face. Jimmy had gotten very still. The man sighed. "How much we asking for?"

"One hundred thousand."

The old man whistled. The woman had traveled the next row back within hearing range. She snorted at the figure and attacked a large clump of dirt. It broke into small pieces with her swing.

"Eugene," she called, "you going to help me with this garden or stand there jabbering all day."

The man sighed again and smiled apologetically at them. He swung in beside the woman. They took off down the garden, chopping like they were twenty.

"Mamma doesn't sound too keen on your law-suit," Linda said when they were safely out of hearing. They were climbing again. Her legs didn't move automatically anymore. She was conscious of each lift.

"Mamma will be plenty keen when she sees the money."

"When will that be?" Linda didn't mean to sound skeptical, but the old man's logic had made sense. Not many winners fighting coal companies.

Jimmy stopped climbing and waited for her. He looked hurt. Angry. "You think I'm fighting this just to be fighting? They'll see the money. A lot more than five thousand."

"A hundred thousand?"

He shrugged and continued climbing. He was soon a good ways ahead. She wanted to call to him to wait up but she thought it best to let him walk alone for awhile. She trusted Jimmy more than anybody but she knew he wanted more. More trust. Only there were so many battle lines with Jimmy. She knew what the old man was asking. Who are you? Our lawyer? Or out to fight the coal companies.

The garden side of the mountain was free of coal devastation. Linda was always amazed at how quickly the landscape was pretty again. A lot of the trees had half-open buds. The sun was almost down but stretched its light through the woods like beams from a dozen airport spotlights. Jimmy had paused without her calling and waited for her. He gave her a small smile, ashamed of his pout. She took his arm in her own apology, holding on tight, and let him half drag her to the top of the mountain.

Jimmy had promised her a river view, but it was more like a come-on for some overpriced apartment.

"Where?" she asked.

"There," he pointed and she followed his finger till she could just make out something twisting and turning like a blue knot. It didn't matter. The rest of the view was grand—hundreds of acres of woodland with a green haze hanging over it all.

"Isn't it wonderful?" Jimmy said, as if he'd discovered it. Which he had.

While he was looking at the view, she curved her body into his bony frame. She could feel him relaxing. He turned to her happily.

"Knots," she said, and he looked puzzled a second. "Like a blue knot," she pointed to the river.

He pulled her closer. She had changed into jeans after they'd made love. He circled her rear with his hands and started to stroke her tired thighs. He pushed his own legs against her. He found the button at her waist and snapped first hers and then his jeans open. She heard their zippers widening and glanced around, looking for a place that didn't look too hard or too slanted. Knots, she thought again, as he pushed her onto a bed of young clover that he had spotted before her, clover that had caught its bit of sunlight on the mountain top, clover that looked like green springs before her body pressed them down into the dirt.

Chapter 8

Saturday was her day to sleep in, but her body still thought she had an eight o'clock class, her eyes popping open at six as usual. She wondered why she was aching until she remembered the clover. Jimmy had made the usual case for staying over.

"I don't think the neighbors still believe in your virginity."

"I just would rather nobody found you here in the morning. The Botts send their kids up here all the time." She didn't know if her landlords were worried that the house had finally tipped all the way over or that they were just nosy. She didn't mention the fourteen year old's reasons.

"Then marry me."

"Not ready," she said, putting the pillow over her head, too tired to read through the script with him. He left quietly.

By eight she was already on her third cup of coffee, having marked a whole set of essays for Hugh's class, comparison contrast essays that were more than unusually bad. A "Before and After," she had suggested and most of them had given her just that. This was before, they wrote, this was after. She had wanted them to detail some change, recognize some significance. Blank stares. "You have to make a point in your comparisons," she told them, not just lists of things that were then and now. "Have things gone down hill?" The phrase was familiar enough. They had heard parents and grandparents declaim it. They nodded. She pounced on a nodder.

"I don't know why," the boy answered. He had the long distance look of the truck driver he was—laid off.

"Then figure it out," she snapped. He jerked his head at that, like she was a rock in the road he hadn't noticed until the last moment.

"Maybe things have gotten better," she said to a girl who squirmed in discomfort when Linda tried to catch her eye. The girl had wide blue eyes she'd made even wider with liner. The startled look. It fit her. Caught, the girl murmured something about some of the roads being better than they used to be— the big roads, at least. The few there were. The back roads hadn't improved any.

"So what effect do better roads have?" she asked. "What's changed with the new roads?"

"Get to shop an hour more in Lexington," the girl finally said, and the class laughed.

"OK," she said, "but what else? What are the connections between the past and the present?"

None as far as they could see. None that she could see either when she thought of it. As obliterated as the landmarks on a walking tour of London she had taken years earlier where their guide kept pointing out sights that would have been there except that they had been bombed during the war. Her favorite had been Dickens's debtor's prison which had been replaced by a supermarket. I could be in New Jersey, she had thought, though the rest of the crowd had stared intently at the supermarket as if their staring could transform it back into a prison.

This wasn't New Jersey but she felt like that guide, trying to make her students see things they just couldn't see. Make sense out of things that didn't make sense. English papers had to make sense.

She scribbled pages and pages of suggestions in the margins, between lines and at the end, sometimes spilling over to extra paper she stapled to the original essay. She switched from red to blue pen, to green, to purple even. Anything to keep the essays from looking like they were hemorrhaging. She tried to keep her suggestions simple, tried hard not to write their essays for them. She wondered if she was doing them any good.

"You think they're balls in a pinball machine," Kerry said to her after witnessing a half-dozen conferences. "You pull back on the lever and they're supposed to hit the lights."

She couldn't even take credit for Hugh though she would have liked to. She was saving his paper for dessert.

"You leave your neck alone," Caroline interrupted her. "You're going to twist it right off some day."

39

Linda smiled at the greeting. The Botts' kids and Caroline were her neighborhood effectively, the only ones who'd think to drop by unexpectedly. Other than Jimmy, of course. Caroline was another good reason not to let him stay over, she thought, not that she'd mind finding him there. She thought Jimmy was just grand. A little high-strung sometimes, maybe, but just grand.

"As men go, he's a good one."

"Doesn't sound like much of an endorsement to me."

"It's not. Most women are better off alone— or with other women. But Jimmy might be an exception. Of course, you'd know better than me."

Caroline had been married briefly when she was about twenty. "A month," she said, "barely back from the honeymoon if you can call it that. My mother made me give back the wedding gifts. I said, 'Mamma, I should get something out of this,' but she didn't think it was proper. I would have thought getting separated after a month would have ruined me for proper forever, but not according to Mamma."

Caroline was a big woman, "almost six foot in my prime but shrinking fast." She shaded her very light blue eyes behind dark glasses. "Blue eyed people shouldn't live south of Maine," she'd say, hating the weakness, hating any weakness. Her gray hair curled up in the Holler's humidity, making it look shorter than it really was though Caroline kept it short. The only times Linda had seen her in a dress was when she was dragged to church by Sister. Dresses didn't suit Caroline. The overalls she wore the rest of the time gave her a free and easy look. They were actually "quite chic" in Linda's opinion. Caroline waved away the notion.

"Chic is for tiny women," Caroline said, "not for big gals like us." If she noticed Linda looking a bit ruffled at that description, she didn't let on. A truth teller. "Not clever enough to lie," is how Caroline herself put it. Besides, she didn't have the time.

"A month?" Linda said about the marriage. "I wouldn't think you'd be even used to each other after a month."

"Well, when you court for five years, you're already used to each other. Anyway, you get used to each other awfully quick in a marriage. Sick of each other quicker. Actually, I was married forty-five years technically, and except for the first month, not a harsh word was spoken between us. Maybe I should write one of those women's magazine articles. 'How to get along with your husband?' Leave him after the first month."

She had had to return to New Hampshire the year before to bury the husband she hadn't seen in forty years. "I was next of kin. He was about fifteen years older than me. Everybody else has died off. Kind of sad thinking he listed me as next of kin."

Neither had bothered to get a divorce, neither had hooked up with anybody permanently in forty-five years.

"You think it says something about the quality of wife I was that he never wanted to do it again?" she asked Linda, laughing again.

"Or the quality of husband he was," she answered.

"Neither one of us were husband/wife material. But we were quick learners. It only took us a month to find that out. I see people taking a lifetime to learn the same lesson."

"I don't think I'm wife material," Linda said.

"Can't tell on the outside," Caroline had answered. "It's a bit like dying. Nobody knows what it's like till they get there."

"And then it's too late."

Caroline laughed, she was always laughing. Linda couldn't imagine what her husband had objected to. But maybe it had been Caroline doing the objecting. "You got your D's mixed up. It's divorcing, not dying we're talking about."

Caroline and Sister had shared the same house for more than 10 years, the mountain's own version of the odd couple. Caroline was the social one of the two. "Always gadding about," as Sister put it. Sister told people to call her Margaret but Caroline was the only one who dared. Even die-hard Baptists who still thought the Catholics all part of some Papal conspiracy, nodded and said "Sister" meekly.

"She don't mind," said Caroline. "She likes people in their place."

But Caroline liked people, meaning she enjoyed them unless they were "downright stupid. I don't mean dumb. I'm not so smart myself that I can't take a little dumbness now and again. But I don't mean to stand stupid."

Caroline was the impetus for huge potluck Thanksgiving and Christmas dinners, and any other holiday where she could scare up a crowd of people. Almost all of them were outsiders, some just passing through. She liked a good time, a lively time, and there was a better chance of strangers livening things up than anyone. You didn't get invited back if you were boring. "I feel sorry for boring people, I just don't want to be around them," she said.

"Except Margaret," she added, "though really Margaret's too mean to be boring."

The holidays were lonely for a lot of outsiders. The natives with their families gathered around them wouldn't think of inviting an outsider. You just didn't do that. Caroline and Sister were still outsiders themselves after thirty-five years.

"Kind of like the temporary tolls they put on roads," Caroline explained to her, "always there but that don't mean they're not temporary. You got to at least have a granddaddy buried in the county for you not to be an outsider. I offered to have mine dug up and moved here but Margaret doesn't think that's such a good idea for some reason."

Some natives did come to Caroline's parties, the more adventurous ones for Caroline talked to them the same as she talked to everyone with none of the special tact that Linda was learning, like a dialect of her own when she talked to a native. She supposed that Caroline had been around long enough for most people to have gotten used to her even if they didn't fully accept her.

"Of course, if I'd been a man, I would have been shot long ago."

Linda noticed she had her hiking boots on—sturdy no-nonsense climbers.

"Drop those papers and come wildflowering with me," she ordered. "You're not doing a lick of good anyway."

"Doesn't look like I am," Linda answered, putting down her pen. "You don't think it's too early for wild flowers?" It was a beautiful day. The sun shone on the southern hill across from them.

"March is tripping out like a lamb this year. Of course it's not too early. Didn't you see those violets on your doorstep?"

She ran to get her jacket for when the sun went behind the clouds, and March would leap "two months back" to January as Frost put it. But the sun was so bright it looked like it had melted yesterday's ice from even the darkest recesses.

"I can't think of anything I'd rather do," she said.

"Of course you can't," Caroline said. Caroline's jeep was out front, her rifle resting on the back seat.

"Maybe I should bring my gun, too," she said. "Just how wild are those wildflowers?"

"Maybe you should," Caroline responded, ignoring the sarcasm. She took her gun just about everywhere. "Though you ought to be safe enough with mine."

"Where we going?" she asked, dropping the subject.

"Away from people, a logging road I know that juts off Route 7."

Route 7, a main thoroughfare for coal trucks, was a little road in most places, a twisty, narrow highway that sometimes dipped down along the river's edge and sometimes climbed into the mountains. Great patches of asphalt had caved in from the weight of the trucks. Meeting one on a curve made you scramble over to the narrow embankment.

"Damn road hogs!" Caroline shouted after one scramble, grinning as if they were on a particularly exciting roller coaster. Linda's stomach felt like she was on those rides. She wondered how disgusted Caroline would be with her if she asked her to pull over.

"I thought we were in a slump."

"We're in a depression, we've been in a depression the thirty five years I've lived her except for about three to four years back in the seventies. But it doesn't matter. Depression or not, it don't stop the coal trucks."

Even in the best of times— and this wasn't one of them—she knew a third to half of the people were out of work. That's why the college was booming. People waiting out their layoffs. But the coal kept rolling out.

"Where does all the money go?"

"Where's the money always go?" Caroline answered, waving off the question. It was too nice a day for politics. She turned onto a small gravel road with a wide mouth that quickly narrowed. About fifty yards in it lost its gravel as if the gravel was a bait and switch and became more like an old creek bed. Brambles reached out to scratch the windows. At least she has to slow down, Linda thought.

"Old logging road," Caroline explained, her words jumping out one by one between ruts. " Whoo!" she shouted gleefully as they bounced over one boulder. "Guess they haven't done much maintenance lately.

43

It must be 25 years since they logged. Thirty five probably." Caroline was trying to follow the deep indentations of some logging truck. Finally the jeep lurched to a stop.

"End of ride. Now we hike." She grabbed the gun and strapped it on her back. She pulled her old straw hat tighter on her head. Several gray curls escaped from the edges like untrimmed weeds. "Hair's getting so thin on top, I need it to keep my scalp from getting burnt. You don't have that trouble," she said, admiring Linda's thick black hair.

"I rode these hills on horseback the first time thirty-five years ago." Caroline said. She had taken a large oak walking stick from the floor on the back seat, more baton than cane. "We young things didn't get to use the few vehicles we had. They were for the old timers. Now I am an old timer." She laughed gleefully at the notion. "Didn't mind riding. Besides you couldn't have made it up here in the vehicles we had. Not even logging roads. They were a big improvement." She nodded as if she expected Linda to dispute her.

"I'd come riding up and they'd run down to get me. Glad to see me. Only sent for one of the clinic mid-wives when things got dicey." She pointed with her walking stick to what looked like part of a roof sticking through the branches. "Right over there. I delivered twin boys. Breech. Both of them. My first year. '48." She rested on her stick a second. " One of them didn't make it. Lungs not right." She kept on marching. "Of course, I didn't come from any metropolis like you. New Hampshire back then was still a pretty raw place, but it was nothing like this."

"It must have been exciting back then," Linda said. She always regretted that she had missed those days.

"Exciting?" Caroline shook her head disdainfully. " I suppose it was though I'd have to get a lot older or a lot sillier before I'd say that. Of course, I was young and that was exciting, but nothing much else was. Most ways, it was a lot worse back then."

"Worse?" Linda's look was clearly disbelieving.

"Yeah, worse." Caroline stopped beside a boulder that been split in two, each of its halves laying side by side like a giant egg. "Picnic tables made to order," she declared and started to pull out sandwiches and sweet tea from her pack. "Tuna OK?" They sat dangling their feet over the edge of the rocks.

"Of course terrible things going on now, especially that strip mining ripping up the land. But people aren't starving, or not near as much. People thought the War was going to last forever. But it just stopped. Like they dropped the bomb on us instead of Hiroshima. Detroit stopped buying coal, stopped hiring. Began to send people back. By the thousands. Like it thanked us for the loan of them during the war, but it just didn't need them anymore.

"This land couldn't support them. Half the mines closed. Nothing for them to do here. Good trees all gone. These not even planted yet." She pointed to those around them—most of them 20, 25 feet tall. "These hills," Caroline spread her hands toward the vista, "were covered with little cabins, lean-tos, any kind of shelter they could rig up. And every bit of ground that could be hoed and corned and whatever had somebody's plow in it. It was like a rural slum."

The landscape was empty now. Linda could see only one lone house off in the distance, though she knew the trees hid more. She tried to imagine it full of the life Caroline was describing.

"I know you're right. The poverty must have been terrible. But it was a full community. I can't help thinking it's a shame they all left," she said.

"A shame?" Caroline was indignant. She jumped off the boulder like a young girl and looked around for her stick. "Didn't you hear what I said? It was a rural slum. They couldn't wait to be shut of this land." Linda suddenly remembered Hugh's Uncle Fred.

"I thought they loved the land."

"Where'd you hear that? That Appalshop place? What'd it ever do for them except starve them? I spent half my time handing out horse pills I called vitamins. I don't want to remember the number of babies I buried, and mothers, too."

"Didn't the herbs and greens help?" One of her students had done a paper on the local greens. She had looked forward to trying them.

"Where were you educated?" Linda became suddenly fearful that she was passing from the dumb to stupid category in Caroline's eyes. "The survivors did what they had to to survive, and that meant greens when they could find them, and they're pretty scarce in January,

45

fatback when they could get it, possum and squirrel when they couldn't. A few chickens, some corn and potatoes and that was it."

Both of them let the subject drop. They had come out to be revived. Caroline dug her stick into the hill and started a furious climb, more forging trail then following one. Linda scrambled close behind her. Suddenly Caroline stopped, so quickly Linda almost rear-ended her. A man had come out of the house in the clearing, about forty yards off. He had a dog with him. He kept it close.

"Howdy," Caroline called. "Out walking the public path—looking at wildflowers." The man didn't move except to shush the dog's barking. "Nice looking bitch," Caroline shouted. Got one myself just like it." She waved at the man and started back up the path. "You keep close, now," she whispered to Linda.

"Public path?" Linda asked when they had walked awhile.

Caroline grinned. "As public as any. All this belongs to some New York outfit. That hombre sure don't own any of it. Wasn't here last year when I came hiking. I'm just hoping those fellows back in New York have forgotten they owned it. Probably just waiting for the trees to get bigger, or the price of coal to climb higher."

"I hope they never remember, either," Linda said.

"People generally don't forget money. And that's what it is to them." They had stopped again. "Look at that," her voice soft now. A field clumped with violets of every purple hue dotted the hillside. Plum, magenta, puce, lavender. Linda felt dazed. She knelt to the ground and pushed her face into the flowers. She breathed deeply. Purples. She spotted a dandelion, a bit of yellow in the still brown grass, but more delicate than any she had ever seen.

"No dandelion. Sort of like a royal cousin to one. Some kind of daisy." Caroline had an intent stare on her face, as if she were looking for something in particular.

"Here it is!" she exclaimed happily. "Trillium. Just in time for Easter!"

She pointed in triumph to a small three-petal plant, the "trinity flower." It was on the crest of a hill. The locust trees above were still bare, the sun like a dozen candles framing the flower. They knelt to examine the small plant, its three green leaves nestling three tiny, white flowers. It was right at the edge of a split in the hills. Linda had never seen the mountains open up in Kentucky. Almost like Colorado. Usually the mountains bunched themselves together so tightly you could see nothing but the one you were on and the one you were headed to. Hill upon hill spread out in front of them with a blue purple haze over spots of green. The pale lilac of early red buds mixed in with a few white dogwoods. "Oh," she sighed, "this is so beautiful."

"Isn't it?" Caroline smiled at her, Linda's "dumbness" forgotten for the moment.

"How could you not love this country?" she challenged Caroline one last time. "You love it."

"Who says so?" Caroline answered, but she was still smiling.

"You would have left it long ago if you didn't."

Caroline laughed out loud at that. "You think everybody loves it who lives here? You think that fellow loves it who's squatting in that old lean-to."

She didn't say anything more. She just plowed ahead, so vigorously that Linda had a hard time keeping up with her.

"Who's the old lady here?" Caroline shouted at her when she had fallen behind almost a quarter of a mile. She waved the stick at Linda to tell her to hurry up.

"I would have thought that was obvious," Linda shouted back but Caroline was already out of hearing distance—or at least she didn't turn back again.

Chapter 9

Hugh wrote:

From what I can understand of what you want—and I ain't sure I do—you want us to compare two different times, and then show what's more or less the same and what's different between them. And we're supposed to keep to the same place, more or less, because you can't compare New York to Harlan, Kentucky, or oranges to apples. Though I don't know why. What do you compare oranges to? Then we're supposed to make sense out of all those changes—trace them all back to some cause, kind of like those fancy spiral outlines you showed us—the ones with all the arrows leading every which way trailing little lines behind them like the bottle rockets we set off on the Fourth.

I almost lost a couple fingers setting off one of those. They make a pretty picture shooting up but have this tendency to blow up in your hands. I still got the scars on the tips. Anyway, that's how I understand you. I just hope I get to keep my fingers attached this time.

The way our hollow was in the beginning ain't really the beginning I saw, of course. It ain't even a beginning Mamaw saw, though from the way she describes the place, it's so clear in my mind sometimes, I could swear we both seen it. Her Papaw described it to her the same way. Like a dream that's so real you don't know whether it happened or not. But she ain't much more than seventy and a whole lot of changes happened by the time she was born. And the fifty years that the world had to wait for me after her birth might as well have been a couple centuries or so as far as our hollow went.

It was her Papaw's Papaw that first came into the valley. The trees were so tall and thick, you could barely see the sun except when you got up on a ridge. Trees as tall as skyscrapers, taller than any building they got in Lexington. One tree would make a good-sized cabin. I've been out to California and seen some of those redwoods. I always imagined that's what they were like. And hundreds of miles of them—just teeming with wildlife.

Everybody says it was rough going in the beginning— being the first to get there and with no more tools than a few axes and such. I guess it was, but to my mind they had a right easy time of it in some ways. Now I can scramble up and down these hills for days and if I do manage to snag a squirrel, he's such a moth-eaten specimen Mamaw says she's ashamed to put him in the pot—and if she does, it's just for the flavoring, not for the stringy little meat he's got on his bones. Daddy says there were deer in the county when he was a boy though I've only seen two, both of them refugees from over the Daniel Boone during hunting season. The government keeps trying to plant some more by Natural Bridge park, but the good old boys gets so excited at the prospect they blast them away before they the young bucks are half-way through puberty.

I don't half blame the boys for getting excited. Those fellows back in the beginning could afford to be calm about it all—sort of like a kid with no brothers or sisters can wait calm and polite for the corn bread to come round to him and doesn't have to be snatching at the platter unless he was just born greedy. Mamaw says in those days you just had to point the gun in the direction your stomach dictated—up if you wanted a few fat pigeons, sideways if you wanted venison or bear or whatever. They hardly bothered with such things as squirrels and I don't know if they even knew how to skin a possum. If they bothered with those fellows, it was probably just what you might call an appetizer.

Or for pure greed. Because some of them must have been born greedy. They sure killed a lot more than they could eat.

Mamaw says for dessert they had every berry you could name: wild raspberries and black berries and boysenberries, and strawberries so sweet you didn't need any sorghum or honey, though there was plenty of that around, too, if you wanted to layer sweet on sweet.

The land was just a lot more yielding back then, black and deep and crawling with big daddy earthworms. Those earthworms were so fat and juicy, Mamaw says, you didn't dare bring them closer than a yard or so to a creek.

"Why those fish would leap right out of the water, boy, and snatch those worms right from your hand. And if you weren't careful, they'd snatch a finger, too—especially if you'd been digging in the garden and hadn't washed your hands."

"Any of those fish around still, Mamaw?" I'd ask, a little worried but eager, too. The creek still ran a hundred yards or so away from our house. Ran right through it sometimes when the spring rains came, or when the government decides that the town folks are in danger of getting a bit too wet and they shut off the dam. They must figure we're used to getting wet out in the hollows.

"Them fish are gone long ago," she'd answer, "and lucky for you considering how often you clean them fingers of yours."

I was glad for my fingers' sake but sorry otherwise. "They were big, beautiful rainbow trout," Mamaw says, the babies a foot or more, the kind that nowadays you only see in those fish ponds they stock for the big-time fishermen, the ones who pay ten dollars an hour to try their luck. I don't know why those fellows just don't go straight to the supermarket—at least they gut and clean them for you there. I guess it's the excitement they crave.

That first land was so rich you barely had to break it with the plow for it to shoot up corn so high you could hardly see the cabins for the stalks.

"Taller than you and me stacked shoulder to shoulder," Mamaw'd say, swinging me up on hers so I could see. We'd be out back in the corn patch, and some years it got pretty high, higher than me on my own two feet at least. But other years, it just seemed like the land was downright tired and wasn't going to yield a kernel more than you could drag from it. Or it'd be so dry, we wore a groove between the field and the creek bed. After awhile, if it didn't rain, the creek wouldn't have any more water in it than we had spit. But up on Mamaw's shoulders, I could just see that corn, even in the driest years.

"This tall, Mamaw?"

"That tall and taller," she'd answer. "And that ain't no tall telling, either."

We only got one small part of the hollow, not more than a couple hundred acres and most of that straight up and down. It don't matter if it is straight up and down, Mamaw will plow up the hillside till the mules start to tip over and then some. Every little bit of land helps when you got more mouths to feed than hands to feed them. Her great great Papaw, though, didn't need for his mules to be half mountain goat. He had the whole valley to plant if he wanted it. Mamaw says that when he got tired of a spot, or when the spot got tired of him, he didn't have to go down on his knees to beg it to yield—or haul up pig shit or cow shit by the half ton so that walking out into the corn field was kind of like strolling through some giant critter outhouse. He just moseyed on down the lane and stuck his plow in some new place.

So much corn and so many potatoes sprung out of the ground that they had to start raising pigs in self-defense just for the leftovers—and maybe for the taste of it, too, I guess, for they sure didn't need the pork with all that venison waiting around just kind of begging to be shot. They still had more corn than they knew what to do with so they built a few chicken coops, too, and got to like the taste of eggs with the bacon. They built a few fences to keep the pigs from wandering off too far, though a few did and turned pretty mean, I hear. But that just added to the wildlife.

Which by that time needed adding to, since a lot of it had retreated a little deeper into the woods. All that hammering probably scared it away, or maybe they just wanted to get away from the smell of pig. I've lived with the smell all my life and it's not one anybody gets used to that I can tell.

"You like bacon, though," Mamaw says when I complain, and I have to admit I do, but wouldn't be above buying it wrapped in plastic instead of raising it on the hoof.

"The world don't come wrapped in plastic," Mamaw scoffs when I say that. "A little pig smell ain't going to ruin nobody. Might even help some people."

I don't see how, myself, but Mamaw never has cottoned much to eating something she hasn't raised, one way or another. And I have to admit our pigs do taste better than any I bought wrapped in plastic, but I'm not so sure it's because we were personally acquainted.

What with the pigs and the chickens, it wasn't long before things began getting what you might call crowded. Of course, it wasn't just the livestock that was pushing things together like an accordion with a hole in its side. That first Papaw Richie had himself about eleven sons and about that many daughters. There's Richies spread out to Ohio and back and none of the daughters ended up old maids. They brought in Cornets and Caudills and Campbells and Bennets and Wilbys and Sallys and Ashleys and you name it, and I'm cousin to it one way or another. And they all had eleven sons and daughters themselves. You were considered a pretty pitiful family if you didn't have at least ten kids or so. And they were all planned. Every single one of them. Or at least they never planned not to have them.

After awhile it must have begun to get right noisy around here with everybody shooting straight up for pigeon potpie and sideways for other varmint. Sometimes that varmint was the two-legged variety. People get on each other's nerves more when they're always in each other's faces, but at least everybody in the hollow was family, and if you're going to spill somebody's blood, it seems only polite you should start with your own. Mamaw says there's always been people shooting at each other, that somehow people, especially men people, need to be shooting something. We're just lucky when it's pigeons.

Before too long, of course, there wasn't too many pigeons to shoot at anymore. I don't reckon that pigeons are the smartest birds that ever flew, but I hear tell they were the most persistent. They kept flying over the friendly skies of Appalachia, probably never giving a thought to why fewer and fewer of their buddies flew with them every year. The folks down below never gave it a thought, either. Till the end. When they stopped flying. Probably scratched their heads for a year or two, wondering where they all went to. Folks all over the country must have had the same problem—putting two and two together—cause the pigeons just didn't disappear here. What they needed was one of those spiral outlines of yours, the ones with all the arrows pointing to cause and effect. I'd have them keep following those arrows back to the beginning. Of course, if they could have done that, they wouldn't have needed to.

The bears and deer disappeared, too, almost as cleanly as the pigeons, though I did see a small black bear up on Pine Ridge not more than two years ago. He looked a bit lost and I don't doubt but what he finally found his way home to some ol' boy's freezer before the season was done. I had my gun with me, of course, thought I don't know that it was big enough for bear. I never expected to see any. I don't think I would have shot him even if I had had an elephant gun with me, though. It was such a great sight to see him looking at me, pretending he was a grizzly up on his hind legs, then scrambling down on all fours and scurrying into the woods.

You ever been up on Pine Ridge? It's a pretty sight. The trees aren't near as big as when old Papaw Richie first came—they're second and third growth up there like they are everywhere, but it's a beautiful sight anyway. You see forever, but you don't see close up. Which is the best way to see around here. You look up and it's such a pretty sight, it makes you forget what's down below.

Things had gotten more than a mite crowded in the hollow by the time I came along. Barely any woods left at all. House and garden everywhere, though I'm doubtful any of it looked like the magazine. There's one good thing about this Depression. The country seems to be emptying out again. Maybe if we get rid of a few more people and a few hundred thousand pigs, and gave the country a rest for a couple hundred years, or a couple thousand years, whatever it needed, we'd be back to where we were when Papaw Richie first came. Maybe not. Besides, I guess there'd be a new Papaw Richie by and by and then we'd have to go through the whole darn thing again.

"Mamaw?" I'd ask when she told me the story of the first settling. "Don't you wish you lived back then?"

"You gonna come back with me?" she'd say, and I said, "sure I was." I wasn't going anywhere without her.

"Well," she'd say, "it might be fun for awhile, but that ain't my time and place. My time's right here. Besides which, you never really know about another time. They might be wishing they were us if they had the chance. We still got the prettiest valley God ever created, and now we got a road to town, too. More than they had."

"The prettiest valley God ever made and a road to town, too." That was her line whenever I complained. And sometimes I saw with her eyes and it was the prettiest valley anyone could imagine—the way the creek wound through it, still brimming with fish when the coal silt wasn't too bad, and the way the mountains hugged you right up close and homey, not like those big peaks out West, and how the trees, even the little, scraggly third growth trees we got, broke into white and purple and pink in the spring time and into orange and red and yellow in the fall.

But other times, especially when I got older, and began to sass her a bit, the valley just seemed used, and tired. Worn out with all the Richies and Campbells and Cornetts who treaded every inch of it every blessed minute of the day. And even the road Mamaw bragged on was just a broken down coal road that wasn't much more than a cow track after the trucks were done with it. But that was ok, because the town it ended up in wasn't worth traveling to anyway.

Mamaw would just look at me when I talked like that. "You're just too miserable to shoot," she'd say. I reminded her of her brother, Fred, the one who couldn't wait to sell off the underside of his land, as if he was ignorant of the fact that the underside kept the top on top. For all his hurry to leave here, she said, she didn't see that he had been any happier in Cincinnati or Detroit. And his kin hadn't seemed any happier, either. Just more lost. Here is where he belonged. He knew it and she knew it, though he didn't want to hear it. Didn't matter if he wanted to hear it or not, she never let off telling him every chance she got. "He's back where he belongs now," Mamaw says, up in the family plot, right on the edge of the coal field he sold off. Mamaw says she'll die before she lets them strip that plot. I know she will. She has a spot laid out for herself—and for my daddy. She has spots for all those folks who skedaddled out of here for the good life. "They're coming back," she says, if only for the last time. For this country is in their blood. It's in their blood and it don't do no good to try and run away from your blood. You carry it with you wherever you run, and it carries you right back here. It don't really matter if you hate here or love here. It don't matter at all. This is where you're at and this is where you belong. She says that to me, mostly, for most everybody else has left. There's a plot waiting for me, too.

"You go on and see what it's all about," she says. "You'll be back."

That's what Mamaw says. I sure hope she's wrong.

Chapter 10

She showed Kerry the essay when she returned on Monday. He laughed at the small preface. "Spiral outlines. The one time I tried to teach them I ran out of blackboard."

He got quiet as he read the rest of it. He handed it back with a shake of his head. "That boy got it worse than I do."

"Got what?" she asked, not really expecting a straight answer. Sometimes, her New York straight-forwardness seemed childlike in Kentucky, unsubtle. "Got what?" she repeated, for Kerry didn't answer at first. He had pulled out his own pile of student essays. He wrote very little on them—a few words at most. Mostly he underlined the grammar errors. Finally, he paused, and looked at her puzzled, as if she herself were one of those essays so hopelessly tangled nothing you said would ever straighten it out. The only hope was for the student to untangle the mess himself. But that didn't happen very often. She was waiting for some answer. He sighed, smiling at her.

"It's kind of an Appalachian disease, one we don't rightly like to talk about in front of outsiders. Especially New Yark outsiders. You just happened to touch directly on it in this assignment of yours."

"A comparison contrast with a little cause and effect. It's pretty standard," she said a bit defensively.

"Is that all?" His face lost its smile and looked so different she felt a bit shocked, as if Kerry had been replaced by a stranger. His eyes looked hard. When he spoke, his accent was muted, forgotten for the moment. "You want them to figure out how we got from A to Z, from promise to disaster, who and what's to blame, and what we're supposed to do about it."

"No, I didn't mean for it to be that complicated."

"Sure you did," he answered brusquely, no irony in his voice. "You ask those questions in the tone of your voice. You ask it all the time. Even the dumb students can figure that out, and smart ones like Hugh hear it in every twist of your crazy New York accent. How'd you let things get like this and why aren't you doing something about it? Look at us. We've come down from New York or Pennsylvania or where ever just the last couple of years, and we've already done more than you people have in fifty years."

"I don't think that," she protested.

He paused. She could see him pulling back a little.

"You think I'm touchy, don't you. Appalachians, skin thinner than a New Yawk model. But everybody hears what you're saying, honey, even if you don't, even if you say it real nice and careful. Some like Hugh there hear it real good. I heard it real good. I heard it when I was a little boy and dreamed of getting away. And I did get away. And came back."

She could see that he was mad. Mad and mad that he was mad. Mad that he had let her see him mad. "You all keep looking for the villains—the bad guys. That's why you just gobble up fellows like Harry Caudill, fellows who tell you who the bad guys are. The Robber Barons. But it's your own folks that count, the homegrown bad guys. Robber barons couldn't have done diddly without the locals —making their small deals and their big deals—never thinking beyond this year or next at most." He breathed again. "A big muddle." And he smiled at her and the smile seemed real—not his usual teasing. "Sometimes we just get tired of educating you, all the outsiders, the foreigners. We all know who the real bad guys are but they pass right by you. You never seem to understand the important parts of the story. We just get tired. Every family has stuff it don't talk about to outsiders. Most folks respect that. But you outsiders keep probing, butting in. And for our own good. Digging into our secrets. For our own good." He pushed his chair back, flipped on his cap and left. The essays lay on his desk. He didn't say goodbye.

Linda pushed her own essays aside. She wondered what she was supposed to do now. Only a month to go before the end of the term. She felt herself being dragged in, deeper and deeper. Hugh's essay had dragged her in some. Kerry had dragged her in further. Jimmy had been pulling at her since she came. She thought of Caroline and her thirty-five years—hating it, loving it. Kerry coming back. She should just clear out. Her roots weren't here. She wasn't one of them. She should get away while the getting was good.

Hugh was coming in the next day to talk about his essay. She had insisted on his coming, though now she half-wished she hadn't. He had avoided her eye in class like Kerry had avoided her when he left the office. Not even a quick wink, a wink too quick, too subtle for her to pounce on but one that riled her every time he did it. She was tired. And Jimmy wanted her to come with him to see some housing hearing that night, the last thing she wanted to do.

Through the late afternoon light, she looked at the hillside outside her window where Spring was making do with what it had—not caring about third growth or second growth. It just grew. Started over with no thought of the past. The dogwoods and red buds sprinkled a delicate mosaic of red and white and purple over the land.

She grabbed the last essay she had marked and began to methodically scribble out the paragraph of advice she had written. She blotted it out so thoroughly it would have taken the FBI to decipher what she'd written. Who was she to give advice? She put the essay down and stared at the trees till the shadows lengthened and she could only make out the outlines. She didn't try to block out the cars and pickups from the view, didn't try to make it all one pretty picture. Even the asphalt was a part of it. She watched as the parking lot emptied out and only her own Tercel was left and still didn't move. Mrs. Nelson started to bang with her mops and brooms. She heard her mumbling at the door, fumbling with the keys, first locking what was open, then opening what she had locked. She startled when she saw Linda sitting in the dark. She liked the pretty young teacher from New York. Linda blinked in the sudden light.

"Why, honey, what are you still doing here? You alright?"

Linda nodded.

"You look exhausted, honey. You go on home and get some rest. You just leave those papers. You go on home now," and she shooed her out of the office. "I'll just watch here to see you safe in your car. Go on home, now."

Linda felt Mrs. Nelson's eyes on her as she walked slowly to her car. She didn't mind tonight, though usually her hovering irritated her. She turned and waved and Mrs. Nelson waved back. You go on home, the wave said. You go on home.

Home. You gave us a choice of words to define. And I'm choosing home. That's where the heart is, ain't it? They put me in a home once over in Jackson county. It was after daddy left and one of those times Mamma forgot where her home was. Before Mamaw knew I was on my own. I must have been 9. That was some home. Me and another boy ate by ourselves out of the pot. The family ate first. We just got what was left. Which weren't much. The other boy had been sent there by his mamma—punishment for something. She'd told him she was gonna' send him to the "home." It's like Mamaw says—feel sorry for yourself 'cause you ain't got a horse, here comes a fella without legs. Mamma was forgetful, but she wasn't mean.

That word home sent shivers down my back for years. Mamaw came and got me soon as she heard. She tore that place up when she found out what they'd been feeding us. Sure wasn't much house left to that home when Mamaw got through with it.

But that kind of home probably ain't what you had in mind.

Mamaw took me back to her home. It was my home, too. She never came out and said so—saying it would make it sound like somebody was doubting it, like "this is your home, too." She wasn't doubting it and she didn't want me to be doubting it, either. Only I did some. I knew Uncle Freddy was off in Cincinnati somewhere. I knew Mamaw had thrown out daddy when he was little more than a boy—told him to come back when he came back alone—without the bottle. Knew that my mamma had several homes running at the same time, like she was riding four taxi meters at once, though it weren't taxis she was riding.

"This really my home, Mamaw? I'm not just visiting?"

"Visiting? You think I got time for visitors in the middle of planting season?" We'd been out since five that morning so

59

I could get some work in before school. "You think you're a guest?"

Well, I didn't feel like a guest, especially as hard as Mamaw was working me. But that didn't mean I was home. Sometimes I felt restless—just like daddy, I guess. Except he never had to go too far to get away—just as far as the bottle.

"Boy," Mamaw said, softer this time, like she was figuring out I was serious and not just trying for an extra question break, "you are as home as you are ever going to get. You just got to believe it." Believe you're home and you're there. I wondered if I could believe myself home in one of those Blue Grass mansions, but I don't think that's what Mamaw had in mind.

Mamaw said almost the same thing to me when I got back from the navy. You might know how it is—you're all eager to get home, you can't wait. But when you get there, it don't seem like you belong anymore. You wonder if you ever did. It don't seem home.

"Welcome, home, son," is what Mamaw said and she wrapped her arms around me which she almost never does and just squeezed till I wondered if she meant to squeeze all the movement out of me, all the wandering. For all her squeezing, though, it weren't twenty minutes before she had me up on the roof pounding some loose shingles. I wondered where my welcome home party was but I guess to Mamaw being home was party enough.

"Where's my welcome home party?" I yelled down to Mamaw but she told me to hold my horses, that a whole bunch of folks were coming over after church on Sunday and that it was my fault for coming back on a Tuesday, right in the middle of the work week. Workweek was right, I thought, but didn't say. I didn't want to admit it but Mamaw putting me to work had made me feel more at home than anything.

So I don't really know what home is but Mamaw does. It's where you're expected to work yourself half to death and not make a fuss. It's where you know you belong. Because you believe it. I don't know that I have a home. But Mamaw does.

Chapter 11

The word "home" didn't confuse Jimmy. He didn't have much patience with Linda's questioning.

"You belong where people need you. Where you can do some good." Where people love you, he would have added but didn't need to. He ignored as much as he could the distinctions between natives and outsiders. "This is your home as much as Kerry's," he said when she told him of Kerry's lecture. It had felt like a lecture. "Kerry's people might have gotten here two hundred years ago but they don't own the place, any more than Mayflower people own the country."

Home didn't confuse many of the people Jimmy defended either. Sometimes it was a shack on the only edge of flat land between creek and mountain, a narrow shotgun with a porch ready to topple over, prime for flood the first hard rain. Or a double wide shaky with rust. Home wasn't something you could replace by giving market value. Not to Jimmy.

For a lucky few, home might be public housing.

The last thing Linda wanted was to be a member of the housing jury with power to evict residents. But Jimmy got to choose one of the five members, the housing authority one, and the other three came from the pool of volunteers.

"People volunteer for that?" Kerry was incredulous.

"People just doing their civic duty. Maybe you should volunteer."

"Oh, no, thank you kindly, Ma'am. Kicking people out of their homes sounds like a lot of fun but I'd rather not."

She'd rather not, either. Kerry's eyes grew wider when she explained the procedures.

"You mean you all have got to tell people to their faces that they better be trailer hunting come morning? No hoods or anything?'

"I think they get thirty days to move," Linda said.

"Well, that makes all the difference. Any locals on the panel?"

"Mostly locals."

"They're crazier than you are. People around here have long memories.

She didn't want to be Jimmy's "man" on the panel. Things were complicated enough between them.

"I'm not a sure vote, Jimmy." They had just made love and he had his head on her tummy. His voice was muffled. She played with his curls.

"I don't expect you to be. But when you see what they're trying to do to these poor people, you'll be as mad as I am." He sounded so peaceful when he talked of being mad.

"I don't always see what you see," she warned again. "Besides, I don't have time."

He pulled his head up and looked in her eyes. "You don't have time to help people save their homes?"

Jimmy might have been left wing, but he was all Catholic when it came to guilt.

The panel was hearing two cases Saturday at the Beacon Motel which stood on a little knoll right at the edge of downtown. The conference room had a view straight up Main Street but from the back so that all the false fronts looked like billboards. Each time she walked it, it seemed like another store had boarded up. This morning it had been her favorite shoe store. They were packing up—without a sale, even. "Mini-mall out on 15," the owner told her, a short bald man who liked to wait on her personally. "Bought all our stock. Wait till they build the big mall." He shook his head. "Next flood, they should just let the water be. Downtown would make a nice lake."

A fight was brewing. A former mayor had been cut out of the new Mall. So had a couple of council members. The current mayor and his people had the best spots on the new bi-pass.

"Democracy in action," Caroline said. "Or which pig gets to nozzle up to the trough first."

"The biggest pig does, of course," Sister answered.

The local banker, Elmer Wiggers, was by consensus conceded to be the biggest pig. He had a big chunk of downtown but had shifted attention to the new bi-pass where the Mall was to be located. Linda hadn't understood how things worked at first. She had actually thought it civic minded of Elmer to have donated the land for the bi-pass. Caroline set her straight.

"Civic minded? He gets to mine all the coal out of the land they dig up for him without the bother of putting things back the way they were. They level a whole bunch of hills for him and they make a few hundred acres that weren't worth diddlee prime real estate. Old Elmer has just civic minded himself to another fortune. Like he needs it."

"Gets a tax break on his donation, too," added Sister.

"And gets a tax break," Caroline echoed, waving her arms, as if the whole point of local politics was just to drive her to distraction.

Elmer was on the panel. He was a small restless looking man. Linda had two inches on him at least. He came from Alabama hill country, the southern fringe of Appalachia, land not that different from Eastern Kentucky. Linda wondered why he wasn't considered an outsider. She was surprised that he'd take the time to be on a panel like this.

"Wouldn't be a pie without Elmer's finger in it," Caroline said.

Jimmy groaned in dismay when he saw the first of the random names, a coach-turned-principal of one of the high schools who was a candidate for superintendent of schools. He had been a candidate two years before, but had lost out at the last moment. He was Wiggers' man and wouldn't think to cross him in any vote. "Almost to hog heaven," Caroline said. The coach was a big man, a bit heavy but in good shape, still. He smiled at Linda appreciatively when he greeted her.

Jimmy lucked out with the other random name. Jeannette Adams was a pretty woman in her late fifties. "My favorite Republican," he'd said when he introduced her. Their third date had been dinner at her house. Linda had been surprised. Jimmy didn't usually like Republicans

"Around here, Sweetie, we Republicans are the reform party, such as it is. We've been fighting the local machine and losing for close to a hundred years." Jeannette blended Southern politeness with sardonic humor. It was humor that rarely cut the person she was talking to.

"You don't always lose," Linda said.

"It'd get too boring for them if we did so we win a little piddly thing once in awhile. That's how I keep getting elected to the school board. Though really it's a mystery to everybody. The good-government vote," she laughed. "That and the fact that my family's been here for a couple hundred years."

It was she who had sabotaged the coach's candidacy last time. Mr. Wiggers was one who resisted her charm and nodded coolly to her. But she let out such a squeal of delight when she saw him that a stranger, a Northerner, might think she was glad to see him.

"She is glad to see him," Caroline told her, later. "That doesn't mean she likes him."

Jeanette and the coach was friendly, too. He couldn't afford to alienate anyone even though Jeannette had been the reason he hadn't gotten the superintendent job. She had somehow engineered the election of a man who seemed to be trying to do something for the schools.

"Of course, he won't last. I give him another year. He makes everybody mad. I tell him, James, you got to feed the chicken a little but he won't budge." She sighed. She just smiled and shook her head when asked how she had pulled it off.

"Blackmailed them, of course," said Caroline, and Kerry agreed when she asked him.

"Only way those boys give up the candy store was with a gun to their heads. Facing jail time. All those contracts. She knows a whole lot she's not telling. One of our home-grown missionaries," Kerry called her.

Jeannette's biggest fight hadn't been schools, though, but condoms. She had put a display of them in the front of her husband's drug store, taking them out of their hiding place in the back where they had rested for most of the three generations her husband's family had run the place. "Right by the cashier, so people can impulse-buy them, just like we do the candy. And me a Methodist of long and proper standing."

She looked pleased with herself. Not too many people stayed mad at Jeannette. She had too good a time in her fights

The Reverend Smythe, or Father Smythe, Linda never knew what to call an Episcopalian priest, was the fifth panel member. Out in the county, almost everyone were Baptists of one sort or another, even if they only went to church for funerals and weddings, their own or someone else's. But in town, the nice people divided themselves among the various sects, the Presbyterians, Methodists, Christians, and Episcopalians. The Catholics were mostly outsiders drifting through. The Episcopalians were mostly outsiders, too, but "nicer." Jimmy wasn't sure about him. He was the swing vote.

"Time to get this show on the road," snapped Wiggers before Linda had time to finish half a cup of coffee.

"We're not your bank clerks, Elmer," said Jeannette, holding her place, and giving him a bright smile. "If we're going to be sitting side by side all day, I need at least one good cup of coffee to fortify me."

From the way "Elmer" flushed, Linda could tell he wasn't used to being spoken to like that, but he held his peace. The coach had taken his cue, though, and gone to look for the lawyers.

The first case involved a woman and three children, two teenage boys and a ten-year-old girl. The boys were accused of smoking pot, an offense that could get the whole family evicted from the project.

"We can't let drugs into the project," the housing authority lawyer said. Dick Brashear was expensive looking, about her age. Jimmy had introduced her to him at some lawyer's function, then abandoned her when he'd spotted a politician he needed for one of his causes. Pretty sure of her, she'd thought but then realized it was just knowing her tastes. She had found out pretty quickly that Brashear's father and uncles ran the oldest law firm in the county. He looked unruffled when she lobbed his pass back at him. His prep-school accent mingled nicely with his native Appalachian. Sort of like Kerry might sound, Linda thought, if he ever spoke in his natural voice.

"Once drugs are let in," he continued, giving each of the panel two seconds of his attention, playing no favorites, " the whole quality of life in the projects deteriorates. It might sound harsh to remove the whole family, but it's for the good of all." He sat down easily as if he'd never come across pot at prep school, Linda thought.

She could tell Jimmy was mad. She felt a tightening of her stomach. She willed calm across the room to him.

"This case isn't about drug use," he started, too loud for the small room. "It's about getting rid of a troublemaker, someone who had the nerve to complain all the way to Washington about conditions in the project." He paused for a few seconds. He looked down, getting control. His voice was softer when he continued. The witnesses were setups, housing stooges or people with a grudge against his clients. He looked at each of them one by one, intently. She felt the coach squirm when it was his turn. When it was hers, he didn't look as if he knew her. "Ask yourself, what's this all about? Two boys smoking pot? Or the housing authority and its lawyers out to get even with someone who had embarrassed them."

He sat down calmly. Young Mr. Brashear looked flushed. He'd just been accused of conspiracy, not something you did to a fellow lawyer in a small town. But Jimmy didn't play by the rules.

The two witnesses against the boy were sketchy: a man who claimed he saw the boy sucking on a joint, "that weren't no cigarette," but admitted he was some distance and had feuded with the boy's mother; a girl who claimed the boy wanted her to try some pot when they had dated. The boy had started dating someone else. Linda shook her head. The case sounded pathetic.

The boy didn't help his case much when he claimed he didn't even know what pot looked like, but it was his mother who caused the most trouble.

"A pain in the butt," Wiggers mumbled, just looking at her. The mother was angry.

"The manager, he said he'd get me the last time, when I got them about the steps that are breaking down. I wrote the letter to the congressman and he sent it on to me. They were hopping. He said, 'you'll get yours.' And now I know what he meant."

"Is it Miss or Mrs?" Brashear asked as he started his questioning. Jimmy straightened up.

"What's the relevance of that?" he barked, but the woman snapped back her answer before he could stop her.

"It's Miss," the woman said, pulling herself up. "It's always been Miss. I don't need any husband. I never have. I don't see that those with them are any better off. Most of them are worse off by a fair sight."

Linda saw Jimmy sag a bit at her answer. Beside her, the Reverend Smythe stiffened.

"But you have three children," Brashear put in mildly.

"You don't need a husband to get children," she said disdainfully.

"Evidently not," he answered. He asked a few more questions about the pot but didn't really seem interested in the answers.

"That's all, Miss Brent," he smiled at her and left his smile on as he looked over at Jimmy.

The case seemed so obviously a setup to her that Linda thought they'd be back out in five minutes with their verdict. Even Elmer had to see through the authority's motives. If he did, though, it made little difference to him.

"The woman's a royal pain in the butt," he said again.

"Some people might say that about you, Elmer," Jeannette said sweetly. "But I wouldn't want to see you thrown out on the streets for that."

He glared at her but didn't answer her directly. "I vote we evict her. She's disrupting the whole place."

"We're supposed to be deciding whether or not her boys smoked marijuana," said Linda, "not whether she gives the housing authority ulcers."

Wiggers looked at her like he had just noticed her.

"You're that new young teacher out at the college, ain't you?" he said. "I know your boss pretty well."

"I know him, too!" she snapped back, angry at the crudeness of the attempt.

Jeannette laughed. "We all know him, Elmer. A nice man. Now about those witnesses. They were pretty sorry, don't you agree?"

"They were good enough for me," he said, the first time he had addressed her directly. And they were obviously good enough for the coach who lined his vote right up beside him.

The Reverend, though, was troubled.

"We're not voting on her chastity now, Reverend," said Jeannette, "or whether she should have partaken of a few of those things you think our store displays a bit too prominently."

"It's very hard," said the Reverend Smythe, "to separate one aspect of a life from another. A woman like that," and Linda could have sworn his lip actually curled, "might well be capable of letting her children run wild. And the young girl, she was quite certain of what she saw."

"She would have said anything to get even with that boy for dumping her," said Jeannette. "She's so angry I'm glad it's perjury not shooting she decided on."

"Maybe she had other cause to be angry," the Reverend replied and Linda could see that for all his diplomatic agonizing he had made up his mind, too.

She and Jeannette argued for another half-hour, but it did no good and they finally decided that the family waiting for the verdict should at least have the waiting mercifully cut short. Jimmy gave her a half-rueful smile and shrug when she shouted out her no to the question of whether or not to evict. He had known it was all over, he told her after, as soon as his client had finished the speech about husbands.

"Most of them *are* worthless," Jeannette said, echoing Caroline, "but I doubt that that was the best argument to make with the Reverend Smythe on the panel."

Chapter 12

Elmer hadn't wanted to break for lunch, "Let's get this over with," but even the coach looked like he might rebel at that. Elmer grumbled that he hoped thirty minutes would do.

"An hour, Elmer, or we go on strike." Jeanette said as she made her escape with Linda. "You see, Sweetie, we do win a few skirmishes." Elmer and the coach headed for a tavern across the street. Reverend Smythe demurred at Jeanette's invitation, bowing slightly. "My goodness. He makes me feel like I ought to curtsy. He doesn't doubt he did the right thing. But I think he suspects we disagree and he doesn't like that. That's why I can't help liking Elmer, the old scoundrel. He doesn't give a hoot whether you agree with him or not." They had ended up in the Mother Goose, a restaurant named for the house next door which was shaped like a giant goose. "Who knows?" Jeannette answered her question. "People get strange notions in the mountains. Wilbur says it all comes down to no zoning laws. Cheer up, Sweetie," and she closed her eyes in ecstasy as she munched part of an enormous piece of banana cream pie, a slice she made Linda share. "Save me, Sweetie." She opened her eyes. "Of course, being a Republican in Eastern Kentucky, I'm kind of used to losing."

The second case was a woman charged with letting her five children run wild. Complaints about the woman stretched back 3 years. Mostly minor annoyances: noise, broken windows, toys used without permission, and some petty thefts, not actually proven, it was conceded, but pointing to her household. Nobody had much against the woman herself—nobody even thought the children were bad—just wild.

"I don't have anything against Miz Cody," one old man said. He was a thin, tall man with rather washed out blue eyes. There was something familiar about him. "She's a good, decent widow." He looked down as if ashamed at what he was saying. "But I'm telling you, those kids of hers. That's what it's come down to. If she don't move, me and the wife are going to have to. Though I don't have the darn'st idea where to."

"At least you won't be looking for a place for yourself and five kids," Jimmy shot in before he let him go.

The woman herself spoke so softly Linda had to strain to hear her. Brashear didn't question her too closely, wary of Jimmy, she thought. Or maybe, she was too sad a case even for him. He didn't seem too interested, one way or the other. Not much of a case. She thought it was all over when one last witness was called.

It took Linda a few seconds to focus Hugh's features, he was so out of context. He smiled and waved at her. He even winked. She blushed. He was the old man's grandnephew, he explained and she saw the resemblance. Something in the way they held their bodies, some combination of submission and defiance. Though defiance had the upper hand in Hugh. He was wearing jeans and a muscle T-shirt. Made for him, she thought, just like young Brashear's suit..

"I stay with Uncle Billie when Mamaw gets troublesome, around twice a month. But I'm going to have to find a new place to hide out. Lady," he spoke directly to the woman, "your kids are driving everybody crazy."

"Speak to me, not to my client," Jimmy looked mad again. Hugh turned to him, giving him a second's appraisal.

"Maybe you can find her a double-wide on a creek somewhere. Her children just need more space. Then when the creek floods, they're get a good rinse cause most of them need a bath, too."

"You think floods are a joke?" Jimmy asked. He was giving Hugh his stare but it seemed to have no effect on him.

"I've never found them to be," Hugh looked thoughtful. "But maybe if you're not a participant, you can find the humor. Hell, man, you can stick her up on a mountain somewhere if you're a mind to. Just get her brood away from civilization." He paused and glanced at Linda.

She looked down, afraid he'd wink again. "Or what passes for it around here. She'll make do."

"You sure about that? Not afraid for her five kids?"

"What I'm afraid of is that Uncle Billie and Aunt Tammie are gonna' move in with Mamaw. You ever see Aunt Tammie and Mamaw in the same room?" He held his line a mini-second, his timing as good as any comedian's. A few of the spectators laughed. So did Elmer. The coach did something with his throat. "Nobody has for twenty years and we mean to keep it like that." The coach let out a guffaw at that. Even Reverend Smythe chuckled.

He waved again when he left the stand, and caught her with another wink. She looked down before he saw her smile. She felt rather than saw Jimmy looking at her.

Elmer started. "She just needs to whip those youngest ones into shape and she'll be alright. No need to kick her out." He looked pleased with himself. He liked confounding their expectations.

The coach jumped right behind him. "No need at all to evict that poor woman. She's doing the best she can. With no man around."

The Reverend Smythe had been nodding in agreement with both men's wisdom. Jimmy had stressed the woman's attempt at church going.

"So it 's settled, then," Jeannette said, happy to find herself on the winning side for once. "We're unanimous in voting no against eviction."

The three men nodded and she turned perfunctorily to Linda to get her vote.

"I don't know," she said and got their full attention.

"You don't know?" said Mr. Wiggers, and he looked as if he didn't like her handing them a bigger surprise than his. "Ain't you dating that boy?" For all his supposed ignorance of her before, there was very little he didn't know about what went on in the town.

"That doesn't have anything to do with it," she said, flushing. "Jimmy knew I was an independent vote when he asked me to serve. That's the way he wanted it."

"Sure he did," said Mr. Wiggers, smiling now as if he'd decided the day was turning into more fun than he had expected.

Jeannette looked at her quizzically

"Hugh was right. That last man who spoke," she explained. "Those kids would drive me crazy. I think it must be hell to live next door to them. Or even within a half-mile of them. Her neighbors don't have any choice. I'd just move. But they're poor people, too. They just can't move."

"Where is she going to get housing for all those kids?" Jeannette asked her. "Who'd rent to her? Even if she had the money?"

"I don't know," Linda answered, not seeing any solution.

"So your advice is flood insurance?" Mr. Wiggers asked, still smiling.

Linda shrugged. "For her or for her neighbors," is all she said.

"I'm changing my vote," Mr. Wiggers said. "This young lady has convinced me." She and the coach both startled. She was losing Jimmy's case for him. The coach was acting as secretary and had already marked her vote against eviction. He started to erase the check mark by hers and Elmer's name. He stopped. Mr. Wiggers glanced at him. After a moment, he started to murmur something about seeing her point, too, about the neighbors. He trailed off. He looked bewildered by the turn of events.

The Reverend Smythe wasn't convinced. "You have to temper justice with mercy, young lady," he said, pleased to end on a high note.

But that left them 3-2 for eviction. Everyone in the conference room, even young Mr. Brashear, seemed stunned by the call of votes. Her yes for eviction was a quiet one. Hugh broke into a wide smile, but Jimmy just stood very still, as if he was hoping he had misheard, though knowing he hadn't.

Jeannette got to Jimmy before she did. "We do what we have to," she said, linking one arm in his and the other in Linda's and propelling them toward the street.

"People have to vote their consciences," Jimmy said, sounding a bit like the Reverend Smythe.

"That's right," Jeannette said easily. "That's what you liberal Democrats preach, isn't it? You'd want to give your girl the same freedom."

"I never set any limits on her vote," Jimmy said, even more stiffly.

"Good, good," Jeannette soothed, and she began to insist that they come for dinner. Jimmy looked at Linda for guidance but she was avoiding his eyes.

"It'll be pot luck unless Wilbur has gotten inspired and cooked up a feast. Thirty five years of marriage and he hasn't gotten inspired yet, but you never know. This has been a day of surprises." They followed her to the house listening to her chatting, knowing they didn't have to say much.

She chatted all through the meal. Even got Wilbur to chime in when she needed help or was away from the table. Linda and Jimmy were hard put to do more than make polite murmurs about the food. But when Jeanette had gone for coffee and grabbed Wilbur to help her, he did turn to her.

" Do you know that fellow who spoke at the end?"

"He's a student," she answered.

"A student?" He poked at the last piece of country ham, then gave it up. "Doesn't look like a student." He paused. "Doesn't look at you like a teacher."

"We get all kinds of students," she answered, ignoring the last comment, "all ages, all sizes."

"Even winkers?"

She didn't think anyone else had seen. "Even winkers," she confirmed.

She surprised Jimmy by asking him to stay the night after Jeannettes.' He looked at her, as if he were trying to decide if she was offering consolation or repentance.

"You're right. The neighbors probably don't believe in my virginity. From what I hear the whole county has given up on it."

Jimmy smiled, his first smile of the evening. "Virgins are over-rated," he said.

"And foolish," she answered. "Or wise."

She lit a candle while he was showering and unfolded the wandering Jew quilt back from the bed. She left her panties on and pulled the sheet only to her waist. She could visualize him standing in the shower, letting the hot water pound at him. He liked the water near

73

scalding. She couldn't stand it. When the water finally stopped, she held her breath, worried.

He paused as he entered and just looked at her. His penis, shriveled from the shower, unfolded, but he kept looking. When he came to the bed, his hands were still damp. They stuck to her dry skin as he stroked her sholders. He traveled down her breasts with his lips till he found her panties and gently pulled them off. He rested his head between her legs and the warmth of the shower seeped into them. The day was gone. Over for him, she knew. He was here with her all the way. The day was over for her, too, she thought, trying to relax, trying to forget everything, everyone but Jimmy who was making small bites at the insides of her thighs.

She could tell by his breathing that he lay awake for a long time afterwards. She had her head on his chest. Her hair covered him like a mat. She stayed awake even longer than he did. Thinking. Appalachia and Jimmy. His causes.

She closed her eyes and tried to will herself to sleep, tried to let the soft rhythm of Jimmy's breathing roll her away from thought. Finally the easy swell and fall of Jimmy's chest rocked her gently beyond thinking into a half dream. Jimmy in the courtroom, mad, pleading. The woman and her five children staring at her. It will be all right, she kept telling the woman. We'll find you a place. She turned to Jimmy for reassurance but she couldn't find him. Hugh was there in his muscle shirt, the shirt too tight for him, split at the chest, pulled out of his pants. She kept looking for Jimmy while Hugh kept waving and smiling at her. Why doesn't he stop, she thought. People will see. He kept winking, winking. What is he winking at, she wondered, vaguely, and waved back at him to make him stop.

But he only waved harder when she waved. Stop, she finally shouted at him.

But he wouldn't stop.

Chapter 13

All Sunday afternoon, people had been squaring up to the loading dock for the food Sister had gathered. Linda's arms ached with lifting sacks of flour and boxes of canned goods. Sister had cornered the market on canned beets—about two dozen crates of them. Linda had been pushing them to a skeptical clientele all day. She had just persuaded a large woman to take a dozen cans.

"Doesn't look too hungry to me," she whispered to Caroline, watching the woman lumber to the car. Sister would have pounced on her for such cattiness.

"Poor people fat," Caroline whispered back. No use rousing Sister. "Used to be poor people were thin and rich people fat. But it's still the kind of food they eat. And it doesn't mean she's not hungry."

The loading dock was in enemy territory as far as Jimmy was concerned, belonging to Big Red, the largest coal concern in the county. They let Sister use it weekends. They even gave her some storage space for dry goods.

"Conscience money," Jimmy said. They throw a few bucks at you and get a million dollars worth of good guy reputation. You shouldn't let them do it." Jimmy was the only one she knew who'd say something like that to Sister. Even Caroline blanched.

"If they get a good reputation helping me feed people, they deserve it," Sister replied. "Coal company or not. People aren't as dumb as you think, Jimmy." That was a speech for Sister. She pointed to some hundred pound sacks of potatoes. He hoisted them up without further comment.

Linda was looking forward to Caroline's and Sister's big Easter potluck get together.

"You know any interesting people, you rouse them up," Caroline asked her. They were resting between customers. "The crowd we got now is sagging a little in entertainment value. Present company excepted of course."

Interesting people. She was surrounded by them. "I know a few," she answered. A thin old woman with a carved walking stick interrupted, asking if Linda could help her with a large sack of corn meal. Linda sighed and looked around for Jimmy but he was busy. She grabbed it with both hands. Caroline came to her rescue. "Poor people thin," she whispered and Caroline nodded.

"You have someone at home to help you with this, Ma'am?"

"Somebody will be around, honey, don't you worry. I'll make do."

She looked like she'd been making do a long time.

The next morning Linda felt like she'd been playing football. No wonder Caroline and Sister were in such good shape.

"You voted against your boy?" Kerry greeted her first thing before her coffee had even cooled.

"News travels fast. Who told you?"

"About half the town. News like that can't be said to travel, honey. It's more like it's everywhere at once. And you got 'ol Elmer to go along with you. Whooeee!" Sometimes, she felt her purpose in life was entertaining Kerry. He stood by her desk as gleeful as she'd ever seen him.

"Were you in the room?"

"Honey, the whole town was in that room. I tell you, we're one big party line. How'd your boy take it? There's speculation that other fellows in town might have a chance." He poured himself some coffee and helped himself to the other half of her slice of toast.

"Jimmy took it just fine," Linda snapped and Kerry whooped again. She thought of his shocked face when she whispered her yes. "He knew I'd vote my conscience."

"Vote your conscience?" Kerry shook his head. He put her toast back, one bite taken. No butter. "Now there's a real man for you. Not like us sorry Hillbillies, expecting our women to toe the line and keep shut. Expecting them to stand by us. Yes sir, a real man."

She looked hard at Kerry. Going too far her look said. "I stand by Jimmy. That doesn't mean I have to agree with him."

Kerry just shook his head again and took a sip of his coffee. They had eased right back into their old relationship, Kerry even joking about his "sermon." "I guess I'm just another missionary, trying to convert the foreigners." He teased her about her "post speech" somber references to Appalachia. "The Tragic Sense of Life, honey, that's a bit too Catholic for Eastern Kentucky, ain't it? Don't mix much with fried food and bourbon. I think it'd go better with your boyfriend. The Irish like a bit of gloom with their whiskey."

She thought of Caroline's interesting people comment. Kerry was certainly interesting. Like a Chinese curse. "Come to Easter dinner at Caroline's and Sister's," she offered, suddenly. He gulped the last sip of coffee. She had startled him. It wasn't something you usually did, she had learned, inviting people to your home that you weren't related to. Another reason Caroline was considered queer. Kerry and LeeAnne had invited her to dinner, but it had been awkward. With LeeAnne present, Kerry had had to be polite. "Lots of people I want you to meet. Bring LeeAnne. Bring the whole family."

Kerry had recovered. "The whole family? Oh, honey, you don't want the whole family. I don't want the whole family. That's right nice of you," he continued, "but I think we're probably going to LeeAnne's Mamma's for Easter breakfast, then to my Mamma's for Easter dinner, and somewhere we're gonna have to work in church service, too, it being Easter and all."

"What about dessert, then?" She didn't know why it was important to her.

"Dessert? Honey, you've been to enough Southern dinners to know that half the meal's dessert —marshmallow salad and fried apples and corn pudding and candied yams and candied ham all leading up to the real point of the meal which is dessert."

"Then how about liquor? Your Mammas probably won't be serving too much of that, especially not on Easter."

He paused. Third time press indicated she meant the invitation. "Now that's a fact," he conceded. "I'm beginning to think you mean to invite me to dinner."

"What do you think I've been doing?" Life in Appalachia was so damn complicated. She banged her coffee mug down on her desk and swept the uneaten toast into the trash.

"Well, honey, 'come on down and see me' don't usually mean we want to see you. Usually the opposite. I have to admit that liquor invite seems real interesting. I think it's real nice how Catholics don't let a little thing like religion hamper their drinking. I wish the Baptists would take some lessons. How about if I mosey on over myself afterwards, walk a little bit off of those desserts and replenish the lost calories with some serious drinking with your friends? You all will have bourbon, won't you?"

"I promise," she said, feeling a bit like she had maneuvered some complicated treaty through the Senate. Happy, too, if a bit guilty, at the bonus of getting him without LeeAnne.

Inviting Hugh was even more difficult. She asked Kerry about it.

He raised his eyebrows. "Why do you want him to come?"

"Because all he sees are so called good ol' boys. I want him to see and hear other people. People with ideas." She didn't look at Kerry when she said this. She knew what she was saying was the truth, but she knew how he might take it, too.

"People with ideas? I thought you said there was gonna be bourbon at this party. Bourbon and ideas are kind of like oil and water; they slide by each other, but they never really connect." They were interrupted by a student of Kerry's, a boy so tall Kerry had to bend his neck backwards. A late paper. Linda looked on as Kerry politely listened to the long and complicated excuse. She had never seen Kerry satiric with students—or if he was, it was a satire entirely for his own amusement and not suspected by the students. Finally, the boy was finished. Some of his story didn't make sense. Kerry suggested alterations to the boy's story that he readily accepted. Kerry nodded as if the boy was being entirely logical now. He accepted the paper.

He turned to Linda. "Now that's another good ol' boy just trying to figure out what we want to hear. A late paper with a good story behind it is like a double paper to me. I hate the honest approach, just a lazy man's approach. And this is the sort of boy you want Hugh to get away from. Hugh's a good ol' boy himself. Who should he see?"

"He's not a good ol' boy. He's too smart to be a good ol' boy."

"Oh, honey, he's a smart good 'ol boy. Your mistake is thinking they're all dumb. But Hugh's just like me. We're both smart good 'ol boys."

"You don't think he'll misunderstand?" She asked, a bit nervous. She still didn't look at him, feeling cowardly.

"Misconstrue your intentions?" Kerry drew out the words and paused. "You're just being a good teacher, aren't you, honey? But what about your boy? Do you think he might misunderstand?"

"Jimmy knows I'm a teacher." She remembered Jimmy's comments about the way Hugh looked at her, about the winking, but she made herself look at Kerry when she said it.

"Well, then, nothing to misconstrue, is there?" is all he said.

When Hugh dropped by her office, she first tried to get him to let her send his Appalachian essay away to a journal but he squashed that idea.

"I'd have half the county on my neck and all my relations, which comes to the same thing."

"We could omit some names."

He laughed. "We'd have to eliminate my name for it to make a difference." He shook his head.

"This county might be half related to you but it's not the whole world. You need to meet different kinds of people, Hugh." She tried to get the preaching out of her voice but she felt indignant. The sun had descended mid-window. A beam of light was blinding her. She leaned over him to pull the blinds and brushed his shoulders. She felt him give a little jump.

"What kind of people you got in mind." He was wearing a Western shirt, all buttons and pockets. It looked nice on him. "We got all kinds right in the family. The sun was still giving her trouble. He pulled the shade all the way down. A cool half darkness enveloped them.

"Educated people," she said and wished she hadn't. "People with ideas," she amended, making it worse."

She felt very shy all at once. This is silly, she thought. It's not a date. "Come to Sister's and Caroline's Easter pot luck. There'll be lots of interesting people. You know them." He looked puzzled. "Sister runs the food pantry in town."

"Oh," he sat up straighter in his chair. "Haven't had to use it for awhile. Crop's been mighty good this year."

"No, I didn't mean that." She paused. She stood up and picked up a pile of essays to look at. She couldn't have been more insulting if she had planned it. She felt defeated.

He waited for her to say something else, but she busied with the essays, not looking at her. "You inviting me to dinner?" he finally said, softly.

"It's a big pot luck," she answered, relieved. "Lots of people will be there. I think you'd like it."

He nodded but didn't answer for a moment. "A potluck? What would I bring? I ain't much of a cook."

"Some bourbon?" she heard herself saying and at least had the satisfaction of seeing him look surprised. The room was passing from gray to dark. She started to reach for the light switch but stopped. She'd have to reach around him. Hugh finally stood up and nodded to her, flipping the switch for her as he left.

"Sure thing," he answered. "What's Easter without bourbon?"

Chapter 14

Jimmy called her an Easter Catholic, the kind that showed up for holidays, marriages and funerals. She only occasionally found her way up to the little stone church built by Italian stonemasons fifty years before. Catholics were sparse in the area but the church was full this morning. Other Easter Catholics, she supposed. The Italians had also built the stark stone bridges that dotted the area, bridges with such dignity she felt a vague surprise they didn't end in some piazza. WPA projects. She wondered what had happened to them. An occasional Italian spelling survived but the local pronunciation made it sound like a native name. She shocked one boy by pronouncing his name in the Italian way. He soon corrected her. The lingering olive complexions just seemed like darker tans.

Jimmy wanted her to go more often to church.

"If I went more often, I'd have to confess more," and she gave him a mock leer. He blushed. She didn't know what he told Father Steve about her, but it wasn't much, she guessed. To Jimmy, she was already a wife. Besides, I just don't need much religion," she told him.

"Everybody needs religion," he answered.

"I just don't need much," she answered. She knew he didn't understand that, but it was true.

Easter sunrise service worshipped nature as much as Jesus and that suited her fine. All of the church's doors were open so that outdoors and indoors seem to blend into one space, especially since the church ladies had filled the altar and corners of the church with pink and white dogwood and cherry branches, with red bud that was almost vermilion, with yellow and white daffodils and daisies so fresh they still had the dew on them. And trillium, Caroline's contribution, she supposed. It had the place of honor on the altar. Linda didn't spot one single stiff Easter lily. The trillium and dogwood branches were white enough.

God's free beauty. Though Jimmy would put a price on it if it was taken away or damaged. She slipped her arm through his like a good wife and he smiled down at her. He had spent the night before trying to calm his clients who were afraid that even the five thousand dollar offer was going to fade away especially since the company had found another judge who let them go on blasting. Nobody around to bother anymore, was the Judge's reasoning. Jimmy's argument about the price of ruined beauty worried them.

"Maybe you ought to take the offer, Jimmy. It's something."

"This was their home," he answered her as if he were explaining an elementary reality she hadn't grasped. "You pay for destroying somebody's home."

The dawn started to gather strength, its stream of light in the open doors and windows no longer tentative, misty. A breeze wafted the flowers' smell over the congregation. She closed her eyes and imagined herself in a field. Jimmy nudged her. The usher had reached their row. She followed Jimmy to the communion rail though she hadn't made an Easter confession. Forgive me my sins, she thought before the familiar strange taste of the wafer was placed on her tongue. She didn't know who she prayed to. She wasn't even sure what her sins were though she knew she must have some. She worked the wafer off the top of her mouth where it had stuck and put her face into her hands as if she needed the semi-darkness of her fingers to pray. But she wanted to concentrate on the sound of Sister whistling a communion hymn. It was a gorgeous whistle, purer than any flute, as high as the highest voice in a boys' choir.

"Practice," Sister snapped when Linda inquired once how she had achieved such beauty. "Practice."

Practice. Unless its God's free beauty. And even that took care. Sheer plod makes plough down sillion shine. Hopkins. No mystery. Practice and sheer plod. Jimmy would plod ahead and use all his muscle and all his brains to make sillion shine, to make the valley bloom again. If the valley could bloom again.

A finch had found its way into the church and flew confusedly above the congregation. When it swooped low people tried to flutter it out the open doors but it scooted above to the high nave of the altar. It was a gentle yellow agitation above their heads and people smiled as it sailed back and forth. Nature is never spent. More Hopkins. She let herself believe. Even the most damaged hollow could spring to life again. Nothing was ever finished. The world was a good place, she thought. She smiled at herself. Her Easter vision. Full of good people like Jimmy.

And maybe Hugh. She thought of Hugh. A good writer. A good man. The Romantics said the two went together. She didn't know. His tale of his hollow moved her. She wanted to rescue him—save him. From what? For what? She kept it vague in her mind, like her prayers. She wondered if Hugh had an Easter vision. She doubted if he had ever thought of such a thing. But he needed one.

Caroline passed them on her own yearly trip to the communion rail. She smiled at them. She didn't much believe in coupling, but since they made such a nice one, she made an exception in their case.

"Come early," she whispered, still chewing her communion wafer. "I want to show you the garden."

"Shh," hissed Sister behind her. Church was not a place for socializing, but Caroline just waved her hand at her as if she were some kind of mosquito.

"I will," Linda whispered back, feeling exactly as she had as a school girl, sneaking a conversation under the stern eyes of the nun assigned to monitor the children.

Linda sat there by Jimmy, holding his arm. Some of the peace of the day was already gone as she felt a mixture of dread and anticipation about the coming dinner. Why had she been so interested in mixing? Why did she need more than what was near her: strength, grace, and devotion? The finch made one long swoop over their heads before finding the opening it needed. She watched it shoot like a rocket out the door, exuberant with the life it thought it had lost, its Easter vision intact. At least for the morning.

She arrived early as instructed, and found that Kerry had arrived even earlier. He had helped himself to his bourbon. "I skipped one of the Mammas," he said in answer to her surprise.

"Which one?"

"It don't right matter, honey. I have put myself in deeep dogdoo for you all's benefit."

"I'm very grateful." His accent had added a diphthong.

"Don't fret none, honey. Truth is I felt more in need of a bit of bourbon than any more dessert. Although I have to admit to a little disappointment. Sister didn't seem none too pleased with my offering. I was under the impression Catholics were more liberal in their views toward alcohol. She said something about this being a potluck dinner, not a potluck drunk."

Caroline was carting chairs to the deck and heard the last remark. She laughed. "Margaret's not what you call a big drinker. The communion wine's as much as she imbibes. But I appreciate your contribution."

"Thank you, ma'am."

She unfolded the chair with a snap and looked at him. "Ma'am, hell. Call me Caroline. That is the saddest hillbilly accent I've ever heard. Just a bit too thick for comfort. Does it come with the bourbon?"

Kerry choked on some of it now as her remark hit him. "Hoo, boy ma'am,— Caroline— give a boy a warning, won't you? This stuff is sipping whisky, not spitting. "

"The accent comes free," Linda put in, "for the benefit of Yankees and other outsiders." She had grabbed a couple of chairs to help. Kerry leaned against the railing, watching them.

"That's right," Kerry said. "Wouldn't want you all to be disappointed. Kind of like going to Williamsburg and finding them all dressed in civvies. When you come to Appalachia, you ought to find hillbillies. It's the least we can do for the tourist trade. But the bourbon does thicken it a bit."

"Don't they try to get it right in Williamsburg? I've been in every hollow this side of Harlan, and I've never heard an accent like yours." Caroline was giving him a look that meant get off your duff and help us but Kerry was ignoring it.

"They're into history, ma'am. Caroline," he corrected himself again. "That's gonna be real hard calling you Caroline. Can I call you honey instead?"

"You can if you're wearing a steel truss for protection," and Kerry spit a bit more precious bourbon on the ground. "This stuff's stood around in oak barrels ten years just to end up as mouthwash. Caroline it is, then. What I was saying is Williamsburg is more into history whereas I'm more interested in what you might call expectations."

"Stereotypes."

"There you go, Caroline. For an older lady, you sure are spry. You should take some lessons from her," he said, turning to Linda.

Caroline laughed this time. "I'll show you spry." She waved them to follow and raced up the hill to the garden.

The garden was Caroline's pride. Their whole hill was on the north side, but she had figured out the spots where the sun lingered the longest, strategically cutting some trees to help prolong its stay. The tall trees on top were still leafless so the sun was almost southern in its strength in the middle of the afternoon. The few shadows there were bunched up close together. Caroline had planted a host of red bud and dogwoods along the edges in compensation for the lost trees. Taken down from the mountains, they were in full bloom, a lacing of purples and whites. Linda let out a cry of pleasure. Rimming the walkways were daffodils and a host of other transplants, wood violets of every shade of blue and purple, small white daisies, and delicate yellow ones, so delicate Linda couldn't imagine how they had survived the trip down from the woods. Caroline was leading them to her chief pride, the trillium.

"First time I've been successful getting one down from the hills. I planted a half dozen of them last year, but this is the first one to come up on its own."

"I don't know how you got any of these down successfully," Linda said, kneeling to smell.

"I don't most times. Ninety percent die if you try to move them. The trees, the violets, the fern. None of them like being disturbed. But if you keep at it long enough, thirty years or so, you have some success." She leaned down to pluck an offending dandelion.

"A ten percent survival rate. Remind me not to check into your hospital, Caroline," Kerry put in. He had lagged behind a little, now sat on the small retaining wall Caroline had built, puffing some. "Hope you did better birthing babies."

Caroline looked at him a second before she answered. "Most times, I did. Of course, I wasn't trying to transplant them. Just harvest them in place."

"Maybe that's what you should have done with some of these flowers, Caroline." He tipped his glass back like it was water. Linda reached for it, but he waved her off.

Caroline had knelt down in the bed and was running her fingers through the dirt looking for weeds. "But I wanted them down here where I could see them on a daily basis so to speak. Can't always be climbing up to the mountains for sustenance. I'm not that spry."

"That's seems mighty selfish of you, Caroline. Think of it from the poor violet's point of view. Maybe it don't want to be moved just for your sustenance." He stretched the word. "Maybe it wants to be left just where it is." Linda winced when he reached down and snapped off the head of a daisy. Caroline stared a second and went on weeding.

"You got me there. I've never been able to see things from a violet's point of view. If you're talking about yourself, I'd say you're already halfway to being planted, you keep drinking that bourbon like it's Kool-aide." She pulled a large soupspoon out of the back pocket of her overalls and started to dig around a locust sapling. After she'd dug a moat three or four inches deep and prodded it with the narrow end of the spoon, she grabbed the plant with both hands and pulled. The roots were twice as long as the tree. She tossed it aside. "If you're talking about most people, about as many survive transplanted as do who stay in place."

"Depends on what you call survival," Kerry said. "Appalachian slums in Detroit and Chicago ain't no pretty arboretum." He reached for another daisy head but stopped at Caroline's look.

"You think a few dogwood trees keep a place from being a slum?"

Kerry finished his bourbon and slid off the retaining wall, being careful not to step on any flowers." You know best. I'm just a poor, little ol' hillbilly myself."

"You, poor?" Caroline's laugh was deep and genuine. Linda relaxed a little. "Well, I guess we better get Margaret to feed you, then. Feed us all." She led them back to the house.

Some more guests had arrived when they returned. Two sets of doctors with wives and children, doing their two year stint in the mountains.

"A real sacrifice, having to live in these hills for only fifty thousand a year," Kerry said to her after he'd been introduced. His words were just loud enough to carry and she saw one of the doctors flinch.

She ducked into the kitchen to see if she could be of any help.

"Nope," Sister said to her offer, moving with the precision of the Army nurse she had once been. "Put those plates over there, please, and then I'd appreciate it if you all left the kitchen. Thank you for your offer."

The "thank you" barely softened the order. Linda knew better than to protest.

"There's something about holidays that just makes Margaret glow," Caroline said. She'd been ordered out, too.

The house was beginning to get crowded. It was a real Appalachian house— a shotgun with a tail— two tails, one added by Sister and Caroline. It led to a large deck around the southern side of the house "so I can see spring even if I can't feel it," Caroline said. Caroline had lived in the house for over thirty years but Sister just the last ten, having gotten permission from her order to live outside the convent. She had lived outside the convent her whole career in the Army.

"Wouldn't you give Margaret permission to choose her abode if the alternative was making her live with you against her will?" Caroline asked. She wasn't intimidated by Sister. "Margaret needs to crab at somebody and I don't mind." The clients at the food pantries weren't intimidated, either. Even when she lit into them for being hungry and being slow in getting help. Sister sniffed out hunger like another nun might sniff out sin. When she found it, she was as stern as any preacher but no one took offense. It amazed Linda.

"It's because it's business with Margaret." Caroline explained. "And hard work. No charity. You don't get offended when someone's just doing their job."

To Sister, it was a job to be done, and if you weren't tottering, and sometimes even if you were, Sister would draft you to help do that job. Linda spent a fair amount of her time tracking down rumored gifts of food or rumored recipients. Her fellow workers were often some of those recipients. Or Republican ladies like Jeannette who had better come prepared to get their white gloves dirty. Sister treated all the vineyard workers equally.

Jeannette hollowed a hello. Wilbur followed her, carrying her famous seven-layer cake. "More trouble than three husbands. But once you get known for a dish around here, it's a life sentence. Take my advice, Sweetie, and get known for box brownies. Put a little bourbon in them and people will think you're a genius." Wilbur laughed and the cake shook a little in his hands. Jeannette looked at him squint eyed and he laughed again. He was her best audience. When Linda had only heard of Wilbur, she had imagined a small, somewhat cowed man. Jeannette talked about him with such amused contempt. But he was a big cheerful man whom everybody liked though he never said much. "I don't give him much chance," Jeannette said. But Linda noticed that Jeannette paid attention when he did say something.

"He's no pushover," Linda said to Jimmy.

"What makes you think Jeannette would marry a pushover? Two strong people can live together."

"Like Sister and Caroline," Linda said.

"I got two others in mind."

Jimmy had finally arrived after working a few hours on a brief. He was still in his church clothes. He sometimes slipped out of her bed within ten minutes of making love.

"Not very flattering," she said to him once.

"I can think of two things at one time," he answered.

"So can I," she answered, a bit meanly. "I can even think of two people at one time."

Before Jimmy could work his way through the crowd to her, she spotted Hugh, baseball cap still in place. He was asking Sister where he should put his bourbon. Linda cringed a little. Sister looked around for her. "What kind of party did you tell your friends this was, Linda?" Linda smiled weakly at her.

88

Jimmy looked surprised to see Hugh. "That's your student from the housing hearing, isn't it? The winker? Who invited him?"

"I'll explain later," she said for Sister was ordering them all to their places. Tables were spread throughout two rooms inside with one spilling onto the deck. Hugh was looking a little lost while Kerry was looking just a bit too much at home. She decided to gather them both and head for the deck, figuring Sister would choose the table nearest the kitchen.

Caroline may have built the deck to catch a distant glimpse of spring in March on the hill opposite, but in April spring surrounded them on all sides. Two of Caroline's transplants, a white dogwood and a vermilion red bud stretched their thin trunks over the deck. Caroline had planted them so that their branches intertwined and formed a bouquet of red and white. Linda's seat was almost directly under them. She breathed deeply.

The group should have been a happy gathering as they sat down to Easter dinner as Father Steve, at Sister's table, intoned the blessing. It echoed out over the three tables and onto the hills. The birds took Sister's part this time and whistled a refrain. The company settled with a rustle and happy expectation at the end of the prayer.

Jeannette and Wilbur had joined their table as had Caroline the last moment, glad to get as far away from the head table with Sister as she could. "The action table," she said, as she squeezed in. Actually, it was the spillover table. Each of the inside ones held about a dozen people, not including the kids. But there was only room for about six on the deck. They made room happily for Caroline , feeling privileged to have her.

Kerry was concentrating on his bourbon. He waved the platter of ham on by.

"How's the housing business?" he asked Jimmy, and for a second Linda and Jeannette thought he was referring to the public housing case. She could have kicked him but he was seated two people away from her and she would have had to kick them first. But he wasn't referring to that. Not yet, at least.

"The collapsed housing business," he explained in response to Jimmy's puzzled look, and she and Jeannette breathed a little easier .

"Oh," said Jimmy, reaching for some ham, "I didn't know anybody knew about that."

"You forget who I share an office with. Ain't much I don't know about your doings, boy." He kept sipping, ignoring the platters of food that kept passing him in both directions.

"You could share an office with Helen Keller," Jeannette put in, "and still hear all there was to hear about anybody in this town."

"Not too well at the moment," Jimmy finally answered. "The Judge they rounded up, good old Malcolm, doesn't seem to see the sense in any of my motions. But I'm working on a new one."

"New motion?"

"New Judge."

"That's good," Caroline said. She was wedged between Kerry and Hugh and kept looking at Kerry's empty plate like it was a crime scene. "Trying to get Malcolm to shut down a coal operation is spitting in the wind."

"He'd call it 'impeding economic progress,'" Kerry said. He reached for a biscuit and nibbled around the edges. It didn't seriously disturb his drinking. "And he might be right. It ain't like they're Diamond Rock and own a third of the county. They're just a little bitty outfit and your boy here," he gestured to Linda as she concentrated on spearing a green bean, "is trying to shut them down for good."

"Not for good. Just till they fork over a little bitty dough."

"A little bitty dough? From what I hear," Linda blushed as she saw Jimmy's eyes on her, "it's more than that. But maybe you all count these things differently up North."

"I think we count them the same way. When you destroy people's homes, you got to pay." Jimmy stabbed at his own green beans and came up with half a dozen on his fork.

"Weren't much of a home from what I hear tell."

"That's not all they destroyed."

"Hoo boy. Now we're getting to it. They destroy the view, too, boy? No wonder ol' Malcolm ain't buying your motions. He never was one much for scenery." Kerry gave up on the biscuit and reached across the table for the bourbon. No one offered to pass the bottle.

90

"Ol' Malcolm," Jeannette put in, "ain't much for anything that doesn't come in plain white envelopes."

Kerry laughed. "Well, now, I've heard that, too. I'd say he had a taste for the tangible. Something you Northerners need might have to develop."

"We Southerners got them out-numbered at this table," Jeannette said. "And I'd say maybe our taste for the tangible has gotten out of hand."

"Coming from the condom lady, that's a mighty strange statement."

Wilbur flushed red, and for a second Linda thought he might leap over the table at Kerry. But Jeannette had her hand on his arm, pressing downward and he stayed in his seat.

"I don't see why," she answered. "Romance and babies don't always have to go together."

"They generally preclude one another in my observation," Caroline put in. "As a midwife that is. I've not had the pleasure, if that's the word, of experiencing either. Boy, don't you want some food to sop up that bourbon?"

Kerry just shook his head. "Weren't you married one time, Caroline?" He turned his smile on her.

"That's what I said. I've not had the pleasure of either."

They laughed again and things relaxed a little.

"Of course, you got a little romance going right here, Caroline. With your arboretum and your trilliums. How much would you say your view was worth?" He swept the view with his glass. They all followed his sweeping arm. The light was almost Tuscan. A photo of this moment would look peaceful, Linda thought.

"I've never put a price tag on it. Some things are beyond price."

"Well now, ol' Malcolm and you might agree on that. But I bet this ol' boy," pointing to Jimmy, "would price it for you if somebody took it away."

"I sure would."

"Ain't right what they're doing, is it? Ain't natural."

"Have you ever seen what they've done to the hills? It is unnatural. Like something out of hell."

"I wouldn't think about debating hell with a good Catholic boy, though Baptists know quite a bit about hell, too, you know. We just don't go into as much detail. Now natural's a different story. Is this natural?" And he pointed around at the spring glory. "From what I hear, Caroline's been stripping the mountains for years. Even knocked down a few pesky natives who stood in the way of her view."

He smiled sweetly as he took another sip of his bourbon. He began to tip his chair back but thought better of it when he saw his table mates staring at him.

"Son," said Caroline. "You're just too mean to live."

"I don't think we're talking about the same thing," Jimmy continued. "A few transplanted dogwoods against devastation. Nothing could be worth what they do. They destroy the earth for a few bucks."

"More than a few bucks, Jimmy. You Northerners sure do figure money funny. But few or lots, it's all she wrote. The only game in town and you want to shut it down."

"Spoken like a true child of coal," Linda jumped in. She had lost her appetite anyway. "Prep school and Vanderbilt can get expensive, I imagine. Every dividend helps."

"Why, honey, you overestimate the family fortune. We'd have to destroy a whole lot more land than we own to pay Vandy's bill. It's a good thing LeeAnne decided to get educated cheap at Eastern. But you're right. I do get a little bitty something."

" Every little bitty helps," Jimmy said. "I don't want to shut the whole game down. I just want to make them play by all the rules."

"If they play by all the rules, there won't be any game. Even the big boys can't afford all the rules. What do you think, son?" He turned to Hugh.

"Why I don't know, Pa. I don't know what the rules are." He'd been sitting back, watching Kerry spar with the table, seeming to enjoy himself. He was sipping bourbon, too, but at least he was eating something, Linda thought. And keeping his mouth shut. He looked at her. The wink came so quick she hoped nobody else noticed.

"Nobody does," Kerry laughed. "They keep changing them."

Jimmy was serious. He had stopped eating, also. "They don't change. Try not to blow people's houses down. Try not to destroy the water we all drink. Try not to leave the land scorched and destroyed." He turned to Hugh. "Try to show a little respect for the dead even if you didn't for the living."

Linda blushed again. If news traveled around this town, she seemed to be one of the main conduits. She felt all three men's eyes on her. She had told Jimmy about Hugh's essay and Mamaw's fight to protect the family gravesite. She had told Kerry, too.

"You all know how many grave sites there are just in this county," Kerry interrupted. "Why there's a baby's grave right near your lady friend's little ol' A-frame. I wouldn't go digging none in your basement if I were you, honey."

"I don't have a basement," she said, though she wished she had and that she was in it.

"Better yet. Your landlords know people who are buried all over the place. Can't stop progress for that. But I guess you all respect your graveyards better in New Yawk. Or Pennsylvania."

"We do and we don't," Jimmy answered. "But if this man wants help in his fight, I'm willing."

Hugh turned his full gaze at Jimmy, still smiling, but openly sizing him up. "It's my Mamaw's fight, not mine, and I don't butt into other people's fights, even Mamaw's. I didn't much care for most of those people lying in that graveyard when they were living. The ones I knew. I don't see why I should care about what happens to them dead."

"Now that ain't no way to look at things, Hugh," Kerry jumped in. "That's a narrow-minded focus on the present. Miz Eliot invited you all to dinner so you could broaden your outlook some. Besides, I hear tell you jumped into Uncle Billy's fight down at the housing hearing. Made a mighty persuasive speech about his rights to peace and quiet if I remember."

"For God sakes, Kerry." Linda was either going to have to get the bourbon away from him or start taking some herself. She did reach for a drink. Jimmy looked hurt, remembering. Hugh just chuckled.

"Now that was my battle as much as Uncle Billy's. I was protecting my peace and quiet."

"I meant it when I offered my help," Jimmy said to Hugh.

"And I meant it when I turned you down."

Linda couldn't meet anyone's eyes. The day was a disaster.

"What's the matter, honey?" Kerry called over to her. "I'm here to broaden my outlook, too, ain't I? Only I don't seem to be doing too well."

"I'd say you were doing real well, son," Caroline said. "You haven't fallen down and you just about killed that bottle you brought, and nobody's knocked you down yet, either. Though the evening's young yet."

"Besides, far as I can tell," Hugh said to Jimmy, "your help wouldn't help much. You can't get them to put a man's house back up when they knock it down. You don't seem to have much luck keeping them in their house when someone wants them out. How you going to keep them from plowing over a grave site?"

Jimmy heard the challenge in his voice. Everybody did. They shifted their attention away from Kerry to Jimmy and Hugh. Linda felt ill, as if she'd overeaten. "Believe it or not, laws protecting grave sites are sometimes stronger than laws protecting homes."

"Hah," Jeannette jumped in. Wilbur was the only one left even pretending to eat. "Isn't that just like Kentucky. Our own sweet home."

"I imagine," Kerry drawled to Jimmy, "that woman client of yours with the marijuana-toting kids found that out. I just feel sorry for that sweet widow with the five younguns. You'd think she'd have more steadfast friends."

"That does it." Caroline was on her feet. Wilbur, too.

"I think," Wilbur said, "I'm going to give your friend a ride home."

"I can drive myself," Kerry said. His peaceful look was mildly disturbed, as if he had some dim realization of going just a "little bit" too far.

"I should drive him home," Linda began, getting up, but she stopped when she saw the expressions on the faces of her friends. They were only slightly less exasperated with her than with him. All except Hugh. He looked real pleased with the evening. She sat back down.

"Anybody want dessert?" she asked.

Chapter 15

Kerry was already two-thirds asleep in Wilbur's back seat as they left, mumbling "what kind of Southern hospitality is this?" The rest of them sat around awhile and stared at each other a bit numbly.

"When I asked you to help liven up the party with new blood, I didn't mean that literally," Caroline said at last, starting to gather up the plates. All but Wilbur's and Kerry's, of course, were half full of Easter repast.

"I hope he has the world's worst hangover," Jeannette said. She looked like she meant it.

Jimmy glanced at his watch. "I'm going to have to go." Ten minutes was up, Linda assumed. Back to the briefs. "You stay," he said to her, leaning over to kiss her. She felt Hugh's eyes on her.

"I'm going to try one of those desserts," she said, a bit vaguely, hoping to salvage something from the dinner.

"I hope Wilbur gets back in time for his," Jeannette said with more acid in her voice than Linda had ever heard.

Hugh came and sat with her as she ate. It was Jeannette's seven-layer cake. The mix of dried apples, jam, nuts, and cloves almost overwhelmed her mouth. She closed her eyes and thought of nothing but taste for a moment. When she opened them, Hugh was watching her face. He shook his head when she pressed some pie on him. "Bourbon and cake ain't the best mixture."

"I suppose you think I've shown your essay to half the town," she said, swallowing, coming back. "I haven't. Just two people. They just happened to be at the same table."

"I guess you can show it to whoever you want." His tone was casual, flat. She couldn't read it.

"I wouldn't do that. I'm your friend as well as your teacher." She had hesitated with the word friend, giving it more emphasis than she intended. He had heard the hesitation.

"We friends?" He sipped his bourbon. He gave her his full attention. "Well, friend, sometimes people get carried away in writing. Wax poetic." He smiled at the phrase. "Maybe I waxed a little too poetic when I wrote that last piece."

"There's nothing wrong in that." Even this conversation wasn't going the way she wanted. She eyed the seven-layer cake again, but pushed her plate away.

"But now you were talking about truth, ma'am. Linda, now that we're friends. And I didn't think truth was supposed to wax poetic." He reached for the bottle. They were the only ones left on the deck. "How about some bourbon to top off that dessert?"

"I thought you said they didn't mix."

"Oh, a chaser's OK." His tone had resumed its old teasing. "They just don't like to go down together. Kind of like a girl I dated some out West. I had to meet her wherever we were headed. We got along just fine once we got where we were going." He smiled at her. His teeth had always been one of his best features, strong and even. "She just didn't want to be seen going there."

She didn't have time to think about that analogy. Wilbur had returned. He just shook his head at Jeanette's unspoken question. Linda started to bustle about to get him some dessert but Jeannette beat her to it.

"That's OK, I've got it. You just sit and chat with your friend." The word friend hung awkwardly in the air again. Linda sat back down. Bourbon seemed like a good idea all of a sudden.

Hugh filled her glass quickly. "Whoa," she told him, but she sipped what he poured. She felt so worn out with the dinner that she didn't much care. She began to understand what was meant by smooth. The bourbon just slid down her throat. With each swallow, she felt the tension in her neck and shoulders ease. The sun was already noticeably lower in the sky. A bit of a chill was reminding them it was still early spring.

She tried to get the conversation back on track. "You know that land is as important to you as it is to your Mamaw. The way you described it. Nobody can wax poetic about something the way you did and lie. Not in the essentials at least." Her voice sounded like a lecture, even to her.

"You don't think so? Not even for an A?"

"You would have gotten an A with one-fourth the waxing."

"Why thank you, Linda." He had moved close enough so that their knees were touching. She didn't want to make a point of it by moving away, but she felt the warmth of his body traveling up her thigh. It mixed with the bourbon till she felt slightly flushed all over. She wanted to make another point about lies and writing, truth and goodness. To say it different so that he'd understand. To say it without lecturing. Like a friend, not a teacher.

"Why don't you come see the land? Then you can tell for yourself if there's too much poetry mixed in with the truth."

The land. She had wanted to see it since the first essay. She had almost invited herself. "I'd love to see it. And meet your Mamaw, too."

"Well, come on."

"No, not today," she amended as she suddenly realized he meant right now. "Maybe when the term's over— I'll have lots of time then."

"What's wrong with right now?" he insisted. "The party looks like it's about to break up anyway. It won't take thirty minutes." His smiled faded and he began to look a little offended. "You can take your own car if you're like that ol' girl I used to date and don't want to be seen leaving together."

"Of course I don't mind leaving together," she said, though suddenly she did for some reason. But she'd have to walk up the hill to get her car and that was silly. This was Hugh.

"Then come on," he said again. "It won't keep the light too much more so we better hurry."

She couldn't think of any reason not to. The land. A way of getting back to the promise the day had started with. She remembered the yellow finch. How it had shot out the church door when it finally found the exit, as if that exit made everything clear. No thought. She didn't want to think anymore. The bourbon was combining with her fatigue.

She felt a little dizzy as she went to look for Sister and Caroline to say goodbye. Hugh slipped the rest of his bottle in his coat along with a couple of plastic glasses.

She got a couple strange looks when she told them where she was going, but she didn't feel like she could back out now. Hugh cleared a place for her in the pickup which was full of empty beer cans and crumpled cigarette packs. "Is this where the poetry begins?" she asked, leaning back. She tried to close her eyes but the world spun too much when she did that so she opened them with a start.

"No, that begins later, honey," he said, and she wondered at that but was too tired to think on it. The sun was resting at the top of the trees, giving them a full view of it. They were racing to beat its final eclipse.

The trip took considerably longer than thirty minutes, or so it seemed to her. Hugh had turned off onto a road that seemed to go straight up at first and then settled down into a kind of steady rut.

"Your highway taxes at work," he shouted cheerfully over the grind of the motor. He had filled her glass though she had tried to wave him off. Half of it had spilled on her in the jostling.

"I must smell like a brewery," she said, sipping in self-defense.

"Ain't a bad smell. Better than pigs."

"Why thank you, sir."

"Anytime, ma'am. Linda."

He finally pulled into a yard, or what she assumed was a yard. There was very little grass but the dirt, freshly raked, had a clean look. Two large geranium pots flanked the beginning of the small walkway. The plants had the long, spindly look they got when sun was in short supply. Hugh parked beside an old faded pink pickup—she guessed it had once been red. It had the forlorn look of a vehicle left too long by itself. She felt bruised and jostled. They sat for a few seconds and caught their breath.

"Is this the road to town Mamaw bragged about?"

"That's it."

"Maybe it was better on horseback."

"Things generally are, but a mudslide is about the only thing that would improve this road."

He helped her out. It seemed a long way down to steady ground.

"Come see the old homestead."

The homestead was a shotgun similar to Caroline's and Sister's, two small rooms, the first a little higher with a loft on top. When she came closer, she discovered a third room tacked onto the second, but lower than it so that the house had the appearance of descending steps. It was in good repair with white paint and green trim around the windows. New lumber was stacked in front of the small porch leading to the entrance. Hugh pointed to it with a grimace.

"The latest chore Mamaw's devised for me. I told her that porch wood had a few years left in it yet, but she thinks she saw a bit of crumble around the edges, though I can't find it, and she's all for ripping it all up. Says she doesn't want to go tumbling down in no hole before her time."

"Sounds like a sensible woman."

"Sounds like a woman who's got a man to do her ripping."

"That, too. Is she inside?"

"Well, now, she might be or she might still be down at my Aunt Mary's. Mamaw?" He called out, but she felt it was more for her benefit than in real hope of finding her. His voice echoed back to them.

"I wanted to meet her." The bourbon was still confusing her some, but she felt as if she were waking up quickly.

"And she wants to meet you." Linda looked surprised. "Oh, I told her all about the lady English teacher who thinks I'm good enough to publish. I even showed her that last piece I wrote." He held the door open for her and Linda walked in. It was warm inside though the coal stove was cold. It smelled of cooking but she couldn't tell what.

"What did she think?"

"She thought it was fine mostly, except for the ending. She didn't understand why I might object to lying up in the graveyard. She's picked out places for everybody, down to the great grandkids."

Linda tried to think of a life so whole even burying for babies was part of the big plan. "You mean she has your spot picked out?"

"Not the actual spot. She figures we can choose that for ourselves— or other kin can. She has just kind of roughed it out, figured the space we'd all need. She's counting on us all having a half dozen kids apiece. But we've slowed down considerable. Way we're going we might have space for a dozen generations."

They had entered the sitting room. "Only nobody does any sitting in it," Hugh said. A large rag rug, full of greens and reds, covered a plain pine floor. The walls were bare except for a picture of the sternest looking Jesus she had ever seen. He stared straight at you with not even a hint of gentleness. A calendar with an illustration of a snowbound farmhouse dated January was tacked near it. The setting looked like Vermont.

"You better hurry if you want to keep on schedule." She flipped the calendar three months forward. A picture of cherry blossoms in Washington greeted them.

"Now that's just what she says. When she was my age, she already had three or four. But I tell her a man has more time, and she ready concedes that. But what about you? You're a little bit slow yourself. I could understand it if you were ugly, but you ain't ugly."

"And smell better than a pig. Why, Hugh, you're just full of compliments today." Her tone was light, but she felt uneasy. She didn't want to talk about her looks. "When do you think Mamaw will be back?"

"No telling," Hugh said and led her into the kitchen.

Mamaw was present in the whole house but the kitchen almost made her visible. The stove looked electric which surprised Linda a little. She half expected wood. Iron pots hung on pegs above it. It was the smallest room of the house, but every inch was used. A pantry had been carved out of a corner, the shelves, only about a third filled, reaching to the ceiling, each stacked with jars of tomatoes, green beans, corn and jams of every variety. A half sack of potatoes rested next to a bin with twenty or so apples in it. One shelf was filled with porcelain canisters. Hugh reached into the bin and took a couple apples. He rubbed one on his sleeve and handed it to her, a yellow apple speckled with green. When she bit, the tartness took her breath away. She closed her eyes and let the taste fill her mouth.

They sat at the small oak table set in the middle of the room. Hugh had opened the kitchen door. It led to the garden. Looking the other way, they could almost see the whole house, the other rooms folding out, one from another like slightly bigger boxes, like a stacking box set on its side. One with windows. Everything about the house bespoke care and elbow grease. The floors shone. The rag rugs scattered looked new they were so clean, except that their colors had faded.

"How does your Mamaw keep everything so immaculate?"

"Too much energy. That's always been her problem. She's had as many as eleven kids in this little ol' place at one time and now she only has me. That's why she drives me crazy painting almost every year and ripping up porches that don't need to be ripped."

"Eleven kids? Here? Where'd they all sleep."

"Anyplace they could find. Ain't everybody gets their own bedroom, you know. Cause I got my own now. Want to see it?" His tone was neutral, as if he were offering her another apple.

"No," she said, quickly, and stood up, too fast. The room spun a little. She sat back down. "Maybe we should go. I feel a little funny snooping around with your Mamaw gone. Women usually don't like other women prying around their things."

"Is that what we're doing? Prying?" For the first time, Hugh sounded impatient. He tossed his apple core out the open door. "I don't think you'd have to worry about Mamaw none. She ain't much like other women that I can tell."

They were silent for a little while after that.

"So what do you want to do?" Hugh finally asked. "Want to see the graveyard?"

"Yes," she answered, eager to get out of the house suddenly. She got up slowly this time and looked around for a garbage can. Hugh pointed to the door. She hesitated a second, then shrugged and went into an exaggerated roundhouse stance, pitching the apple well into the yard.

"Good arm," he whistled and touched her bicep. She laughed, embarrassed by the gesture.

He led the way out, still carrying the bourbon and cups. There was only a little left in the bottle. She shook her head when he offered. He tossed the cups by the door and shoved the bottle into the side pocket of his jeans. They followed the creek line up the hill. The shadows were deeper now. "We'll keep the light if we hurry," Hugh said and quickened his stride. The creek was full, almost tipping over the banks. He took her hand when they had to cross it, keeping her steady as she stepped from flat boulder to flat boulder, the only bridge over. They came to a little clearing and she was surprised at how high they had climbed. They could see the house and garden beneath them. She hadn't noticed that the house was set on a little knoll which must have kept it from being flooded in an ordinary year. The rains had already been heavy this spring.

"About every seven years the good Lord, as Mamaw say, sees fit to send us a flood. Due for another one soon."

"What do you do then?" she asked.

"You just open the front and back doors and let the water in one way and out the other. If you don't the creek might take the whole house."

She looked at him skeptically. "Waxing poetic?"

He looked back at her open faced, the picture of honesty. "No, Ma'am."

"It must be terrible," she said, convinced.

"Not that bad. Last time was about five, six years ago. Kept Mamaw scrubbing mud for a month. That was some spring cleaning. Only thing was, it ruined the garden. Mamaw felt that worse than the house."

The garden stretched for more than an acre beyond the kitchen door, though only a third of it was planted. The rest was turned over, under, tilled ready for the corn, tomatoes, green beans and potatoes that had to wait a few weeks for the frost danger to pass. But even this early, the garden showed the signs of considerable work. What could be done had been done. Rows of baby lettuce, kale, mustard greens, turnips and even some onions lay before them, some of the lettuce almost harvest ready. It could be Vermont, she thought, but it was different somehow. She wished she hadn't turned the calendar. Maybe Mamaw wasn't interested in the date. She had her own calendar.

"You help?" she asked, pointing to the garden.

"As little as possible. Don't need to. It's only about a third of what it used to be. She finally got tired of throwing away most of what she growed. Even the pigs couldn't eat anymore. This ain't hardly enough work to raise a sweat as far as Mamaw's concerned."

It looked enough to her. She was sweating now as they kept climbing, the earlier chill forgotten. The light only found its way in small fingers in the woods and she was grateful for Hugh's hand in hers as he led her upwards. She paused to catch her breath. Quietly, Hugh waited by her side. He pulled the bottle from his pocket and took another swig. When she was ready he reached for her, his two hands on her waist, and before she knew it, he was swinging her over a small ravine, an opening in the trail she could barely see. It was like the rush of a roller coaster as her feet flew upwards and then down back to the ground. He kept one arm on her waist for awhile until the trail narrowed again, then slipped his hand into hers and kept pulling. His grip hurt her hand.

"How does everybody get up here for funerals?" She was gasping for air.

"Well, the main attraction's carried. The others walk. There's an old wagon road for those who can't. But this is prettier." He didn't pause when he talked. "Of course, there's a coal road now on the other side. But you'll see for yourself."

They had finally reached the top. It opened up into a large plateau, the biggest flat or nearly flat place she had seen for a long time. About thirty or so grave markers, most just round rocks with a few carved words on them, were lined neatly in one section of the plateau. The graves covered less than a third of the whole, the section nearest the edge which formed almost a cliff. Plenty of room for future generations.

They walked to the edge. Below was the view she had imagined before she came to Appalachia, the season's delicate greens mixing with the ghostly whites of dogwood and wild apple. It was still light enough to see. The purple of the red bud threaded through the scene like the stitching of a quilt.

"It's wonderful. What a place to lie for eternity."

"It's alright, I guess. I don't know about eternity, though. They might have something to say about that," and he pointed to the other side of the plateau. Even from this distance, she could see the destruction. A high wall of dirt and trees marked the other side, like the high water mark of some devastating flood. In front of the wall was flat, scraped land. "Maybe they just got to lie up facing away so we get the pretty view. You reckon?" And he pulled her closer to the edge of the cliff. Dead trees were stuck in the mounds of dirt like upended telephone poles.

She pulled her hand free. "But your Mamaw didn't sign away this land. They can't come over here."

"It ain't all that clear what they can do. They claim Uncle Freddy included this land when he signed away his rights. Truth is, this land with the graveyard was held in common by everybody. Nobody was gonna do anything but lie in it for eternity. Things are in a little bit of a muddle. As usual." He spit over the edge. His voice was cold, hard. As if he wasn't talking to her. He stared at the devastation for a moment. When he turned back to her, he stared at her with the same eyes.

The chill had come back. She wished she had brought a jacket.

"That's why you need to get Jimmy to help."

"I'll guess I'll decide about that," he said, and his voice was so hostile she decided not to press it. She had sat on one of the oldest tombstones on the lot. "Some great great great uncle," said Hugh, sitting by her. The stone had tipped over and sunk almost into the ground. It felt cool and smooth on her legs. He put his arm around her waist and she let him, hoping to bring him back from the scene in front of them. A kiss on a tombstone with her favorite student didn't seem like such a big deal. One kiss and then they'd head on back.

Hugh tilted the bottle of bourbon up, draining the last of it. He took the bottle then and with his own roundhouse pitch shot it out over the cliff. They could hear it shattering far below.

"Hugh!" She was shocked.

"Oh, excuse me, ma'am. Littering. That's a no no, ain't it?"

"Why would you do such a thing? In a place like this?" She tried to remove his arm but he held tight. She didn't feel like a kiss anymore.

"Don't turn school-marm on me, Linda. You think a little bit of glass is gonna matter when those boys get done with it?" He pointed over to the stripped field.

"You don't have to add to it." She felt indignant, as if Hugh himself had stripped the land.

"I don't see why not. Why let those boys have a clear field? But then I'm just a hillbilly and don't understand these things much." Kerry's line. She was tired of it. He had moved closer to her on the stone. He put his other arm around her.

She looked at him. She didn't know why she felt surprised. Things were moving faster than she wanted.

"No, Hugh." She tried to push his arms away.

"Now why not? Ain't this a pretty view? Poetry. You like poetry, don't you? This is the real thing. No waxing." He had pulled her close to him. The gravestone was the last in the row, only a few feet from the ravine. Pulling away might tumble them over.

"No, Hugh, " she said again, and attempted to get up, but he held her in place. He was pressing her down onto the rock. Somehow he had pinned her legs with his. His weight pressed so hard she could feel the carving on the stone. The edges of the old letters cut into her back. "Hugh," she yelled, sure that his shouted name would bring him back. She couldn't see his face in the near dark. He had trapped her arms to her side. She tried to hit him but her close held arms made only thumping taps on his chest.

"Hugh, let me up. Stop it." She was screaming now, frantic.

He had taken one large breast from her bra. He held it in his free hand and looked at it. "Come on, honey. You know you don't want me to stop." His voice was foreign to her. Scraped. He talked slowly as if there was no hurry. None at all. "You'll just like that 'ol girl I dated. Don't want to be seen going where you want to go. Why'd you come on up here if you didn't? You take a walk with a good ol' boy and you know what to expect."

He dropped her breast and left the other alone as if he'd seen all he needed. He started to work her skirt up to her waist. The cold surface of the stone traveled up her thighs. She wished she could see his face. She freed one arm and started to pound at his head. He let her.

"Hugh, stop it. You're not a good ol' boy," she yelled. "You're better than that."

"Sure I'm a good ol' boy, honey," and she could feel blood flowing from his nose where she had connected. "We're all good ol' boys around here," and even in her panic, she remembered Kerry saying the same thing.

"I'm not better than anybody," Hugh said. "You just keep trying to get me above my raisin.' I am gonna fuck me an English teacher, though. That's something." He had hold of her panties when he said that and he ripped them off with one pull, with the same kind of gesture with which he had thrown the bottle over the grave stone. She felt the rip and the sting of the rip scratched her thigh and she knew it was too late. She felt him fumbling with his fly and she kept punching at him but she knew it was too late.

She felt another rip as he rammed into her and her head hit the stone, and tears of pain flushed her eyes but she didn't feel like crying. She let her free hand fall to her side as she watched him over her, pulling in and out, each thrust in a sear of pain that brought her back for a mini-second. She felt her eyes clouding over like the fog climbing the walls of a hollow. "Hugh," she said, calling for his help, certain he would protect her if only he heard. "Hugh," she called again before she slipped into a kind of sleep, a sleep she kept waking from, wondering who it was above her, who it was that looked so vaguely familiar as if she ought to have known him. But she didn't.

Chapter 16

1884. She traced the number with her finger. Her cheek lay right beside it. The outlines of the number had been filled in with moss and was impossible to read when standing above it. A hundred years. Great great great uncle so and so had been dead a hundred years and his great great great nephew had just raped her on his tombstone. The moss felt cool to her cheek. Tiny purple flowers were hidden beneath the green surface. How sweet, she thought. I never would have spotted them.

She sat up. Her skirt was still around her waist and she pulled it down, looking around for her panties.

"Ain't much left of them," Hugh said, holding them out for her. Hugh here? she thought for a second. That's right. Hugh's here. He was standing over her, looking very serious. She had never seen him looking so serious. His shirt had dark red stains. Blood, she realized. How had that happened? She looked at her own hand. Blood, too. He offered her a hand up.

She shook her head.

He put his hand down. It was dark. No moon. She could only see the outlines of things. The last of Easter. She looked down at the stone. She stroked the cool moss. I'll just lie back down a second, she thought.

"Feels like rain. We'll have to hurry. We don't want to stumble over that trail in the dark and rain, too."

She just looked at him. She tried to smile to show him she understood.

"We have to get going," he said again and she nodded, proud of the effort. We have to get going.

He looked puzzled at her silence, but turned to go. "Follow me. Don't lose sight of me now or you'll be wandering these mountains for days." He didn't offer to take her hand.

She waited till he started down and then began to follow. He paused about ten yards down to make sure she was there. She stopped when he stopped, as if there was a pact between them—so much distance. She watched the silver visor on his cap. She had never noticed it before. It shone like a coal lamp leading her into the dark. Mountain dark. Her dress caught on blackberry brambles and she tugged at it . She ripped it free and it stuck again. She pulled at the brambles . The thorns pricked her fingers. The pain was like little knives stabbing at her. She watched as blood bubbled up and reached to suck them but not before some drops had spilled on the coral front of her dress. She looked down at her dress. Her Easter dress. Ruined now.

Hugh had disappeared. She felt a moment's panic. Hugh, she tried to call but no sound came. She heard him coming back. He stuck his head around the bend.

"You OK?" he yelled across the distance.

OK, she nodded, and he turned again. She followed, trying to keep up. He was going so fast. She didn't see the ravine he had flown her over and she tumbled into it. She rolled down into the bushes that had settled into the cracked path. It wasn't deep, but when she scrambled up the brambles tore at her legs and arms. One branch whipped across her face. When she found the path, Hugh was gone again. But she remembered the way down now.

No lights were on in the house yet.

Hugh was waiting by the door. He startled at her torn dress and bloody face. He had washed his. "I guess Mamaw decided to stay the night with Aunt Mary. Why don't you come on in and get cleaned up?"

A bath, she thought. I can't take one here, she said. Or meant to say. She started to walk down the road by herself.

"Where you going?" Hugh's voice was shouting. Why was he shouting? This was the road to town, wasn't it? She tried to remember how far. Very far. But that was OK. She heard Hugh jump into the pickup. He was following her, yelling something. He pulled beside her but she kept on walking. It felt good to walk on the open road. No branches, no brambles. She saw a small bit of the moon sticking above the trees. The pickup pulled ahead of her and the passenger door opened, blocking her way.

"Get on in, for Christ sakes. Get on in."

She shook her head politely. It was so nice to walk. Why didn't he understand? The cool air felt so good on her scratches. She pushed the door aside and continued walking. She heard him curse. The pickup followed her like a big dog she couldn't lose—making so much noise. She wished it'd go away.

She stopped. The road split in two. Which way she wondered, but couldn't remember. She looked again at the pickup's open door as if she had just discovered it. She pulled herself up like she had pulled herself out of the ravine. He reached across her to shut the door and she shuddered as his arm brushed her breasts. The door handle cut into her side.

"Don't worry. I'm not going to touch you."

The pickup on the rutted road pitched them up and down like an aging carnival ride. She missed the peace of the walk. She looked for the moon, but they curved and twisted so she never caught more than a glimmer of it. They rode in silence till they hit the cutoff. On the black topped road, the noise of the motor was less, the wind soothing through the open window. She felt like they were gliding through the waves now. She felt him turn towards her.

"Look," he said, "I got kind of carried away up there, didn't I? I guess graveyards and bourbon don't mix, either."

Graveyards and bourbon. It sounded like a song title, she thought. A country song.

"I sure didn't mean for this to happen. I mean not the way it did. I thought maybe things would go a little easier."

Smooth and easy, she thought. Like the bourbon.

"I'm sorry it got rough up there. But nobody needs to know anything about it."

Know what? Graveyards and bourbon? She looked at him now, puzzled.

"You want to protect your reputation," he said slowly as if he was talking to a child.

She nodded. Her reputation.

"You gonna' say anything?" Hugh said. "You know I wasn't alone up there. It takes two to tangle. Say something," he yelled.

She moved her mouth. She didn't seem able to say anything. They were approaching her hill. He was slowing down.

"Let me out," she said, finding a voice, and had the door open before he could screech to a halt. She leaped down to the ground and fell one last time to her knees.

"Jesus!" she heard him shout. "You all right?" but she was silent again. She climbed to her feet. "You all right?" he asked again. She moved to the side of the road under the cover of a large poplar. Little green buds were just opening. She looked for the moon again. It was half way out of the trees already. She listened to the squeal of his tires as he gunned the motor down the road.

Jesus! The word echoed in the night. The birds had retired for the evening, and it was too early in the spring for other sounds. She remembered the wall of sound the cicadas had made the summer before. A solid sound—like the sound a waterfall makes—or the ocean. She missed the ocean. Now only the word Jesus and the dim fading of the pickup broke the silence. *Jesus! He has risen.* The pain in her knees made her look down. Easter's over, she thought.

She paused to catch her breath by Sister's and Caroline's house. The lights were still on. Cleaning up. She should have stayed and helped. The pain in her knees lashed at her like a wave. "Oh," she moaned and didn't know how she was going to make it to the top of the hill, to her little tilted A-frame. She sat down on the road.

Caroline's dog, Missy, was the first to spot her and came racing over. She brought the other half dozen dogs who hung around with her, all of them bellowing warning or welcome. But Missy sensed before she reached the figure sitting so strangely in the road that she knew her. She knew her smell before she recognized her face. The figure sat so still, only her hands fluttering an invitation to them. She beat the other dogs in the race to the familiar hands that started to scratch deliciously behind her ears. The other dogs crowded in, trying to grab the caresses for themselves, but one hand still kept scratching at Missy's ears, murmuring sweet low sounds.

Such sweet dogs, Linda thought, her legs stretched out before her.

"Sweet Jesus!" Caroline said, echoing Hugh's last words. "What in the name of God happened to you?"

She looked up. Caroline sounded scared, too. She tried to smile one last time but her knees hurt so. Sister had followed Caroline to the door.

"Help her up," said Sister, and together they half carried, half led her inside.

"I want a bath," were the first words she could speak.

"A bath?" Caroline started to say something more, but Sister put her finger to her lips.

"Certainly, you can have a bath," Sister said, and Linda was surprised at the peculiar gentleness to her tone. "But just lie down here," she continued, directing her to a bed that Caroline had hurriedly pulled the quilt back from. She had always admired that quilt, a double wedding ring in beautiful reds and yellows.

She felt Sister run her fingers lightly over her body. She began to shiver.

"I'm cold," she said, and they pulled the quilt up over her.

"Any broken bones?" Caroline asked, as Sister motioned for her to wait. She was taking a pulse.

"No broken bones. Shock." Caroline went to get another quilt. It was a vivid quilt, full of greens and purples. It hurt her eyes.

"Drunkard's Path," Linda murmured.

"What?" Sister leaned in closer to catch her words.

"Drunkard's Path," she said again, pointing to the quilt as she closed her eyes.

Chapter 17

When she awoke she discovered that someone had changed her clothes, put her in a nightgown and washed and dressed her wounds. She only vaguely remembered any of it. Sister and Caroline coming in periodically throughout the night, gently waking her, checking.

"We should have been able to manage. Between the two of us, we have almost a century's worth of nursing experience," Caroline explained when she wondered at it. "Of course you don't remember anything. When you started to wake up, I gave you a shot. Another advantage to having old nurses for neighbors." The curtains had been opened. The sun made a circle of light on the bed. Caroline's bed, she realized.

"Where did you sleep?" She heard rather than saw Caroline moving busily around the room, opening drawers, rearranging something on the bureau. A small brown water stain on the bedroom ceiling caught her eye. It was shaped like a child's drawing of the sun, with a circle and spokes for the rays. But all in brown.

"On the sofa bed in the living room. Now I realize why our houseguests don't linger longer than a day or so. That thing's headed for the dump as soon as I can get a truck. The little buttons poking you in the back are bad enough, but what in heaven's name is the purpose of that metal bar cutting your mid-section in half? I've been in dentists' chairs that were three times as comfortable." Caroline chatted lightly as if Linda had just dropped by for a morning's chat.

Linda sat up straight. "School!"

"You just lie back down, you're not going anywhere. It's already been taken care of. Nobody expects you for a couple days." Caroline pressed her shoulders gently and Linda lay back down.

"What did you tell them?" Her voice was quiet. She looked for her little brown sun.

"We didn't know what to tell them so we just told them 'under the weather.' We figured you could fill in any details you wanted to later."

"Under the weather?" A soft breeze from that weather blew in now. Caroline had lined her garden up so that she could view it from her bed. She could see the forsythia trembling slightly in the breeze. Their yellow seemed too bright to be real.

"That's about it, physically at least. Of course, we weren't equipped to give you a thorough examination, you'd have to go up to the hospital for that though I don't know that they could do much better." Sister and Caroline were both contemptuous of the local hospital. "But mostly what we found was a mass of scratches. Did you go rolling in a briar patch? And a few minor contusions. You had a little bump on the back of your head, too. But we kept waking you and you seemed responsive so it's probably nothing to worry about. Probably giving you a little headache this morning."

"Especially with you not giving her a minute's peace." Sister had bustled into the room with a tray laden with orange juice, tea, and toast. "You just stay where you are," she ordered, her voice still gentle but with some of the no-nonsense quality back in it. "That bump on your head might have been a concussion though it doesn't seem to be. No use taking any chances for a day or so."

Linda lay back as Sister took her pulse.

"Better, but still a bit erratic. We better have Doctor Bowen come look." Dr. Bowen had been one of the guests at the Easter dinner.

"No," she said. She didn't want anyone else to see her.

Sister looked at her hard. "If I say a doctor's needed, he's needed."

"Please," she said. "I'm feeling so much better."

"Now who's not giving her any peace?" Caroline interrupted. "Why don't we wait for a few hours, see how she's coming along?"

Sister finally nodded in agreement.

After that both of them left her, and she lay watching Caroline's garden. She lay very still, shifting her gaze to her little brown sun when the garden became too rich for her eyes, too vivid. Too loud. She drifted into sleep without thinking, the soft sounds in the house coming to her like the distant sounds the city made at night in her bedroom at her parent's 11th floor apartment. When she woke again, there was some broth steaming in a bowl along with a small salad. Sister watched steadily until she had swallowed a few sips and nibbled at the salad and then went on about her duties. Duties. She had duties, too. But she lay there, not even thinking of getting up. She listened to one bird trilling insistently. Even the birds.

"Thank God you're here to help us eat this ham," Caroline said as she entered. "What's that joke about eternity? Two people and a ham." The sunlight had disappeared from the bed. The colors in the garden were softer. Linda looked at her plate. They had cut the ham into bite size pieces. Nobody had cut her food for her since she was six.

"I know you're wondering what happened?" she said.

"Only if you want to tell us," Caroline blinked, caught off-guard.

"I don't know if I want to tell you."

"Then wait until you're sure," and Linda saw that she was a little nervous, as if she wasn't so sure herself that she wanted to hear.

"I'll wait then."

"You just get a good night's sleep."

Linda felt a small surprise. Night again? She nibbled at the ham, then put her fork down. "Not much help with eternity." She smiled and felt another surprise that she could joke. "But where are you going to sleep? Not on that couch again." She started out of her bed.

"Whoa, young lady," Caroline said, and Linda lay back down at her look. "You want to get me in Dutch with Margaret? I'll be just fine. I put the mattress on the floor. 'Just like a hippie,' Margaret said when she saw me. I just wish I had some incense to burn. That would really set her off."

"I think I have some," Linda said, feeling tired again, as if the conversation and the little bit of ham had been a day's work.

"Well maybe I'll run up later and get me some," were the last words she heard and then she was asleep again.

When she awoke again Jimmy was sitting on her bed, waiting for her to open her eyes. It was daylight but cloudy. They had closed the window to a mere crack in case of rain. He had been in court in Frankfort all of Monday. She had known that— had known that she had a day's respite. She had known, too, that it wouldn't last.

"How are you? What happened?" Jimmy wouldn't wait for her to be ready. He was ready. She felt his eyes locked onto her face.

"I'm fine," she said, answering the first question.

"What happened?" he asked again.

"I don't want to talk about it now," she said, hoping against hope that Sister and Caroline would have told him to hold off questioning. If they had, it didn't matter.

"The hell you don't. I'm sorry." He paused. "We've already lost two days. You need to tell me what happened."

She turned her face to the wall. It was a plain white wall that gave her nothing.

"They should have taken you to the hospital. I don't care what they think about that place." Jimmy's voice was controlled. He was holding his temper in check.

"I didn't want to go to the hospital."

"It doesn't matter what you wanted." He was almost yelling. He sprang from the bed so quickly she bounced softly in his wake. "You weren't in any condition to say what you wanted." He grew quieter. "Tell me what happened."

She wouldn't answer, but kept her face turned away. The white wall had a sheen. She could see her own face vaguely reflected at her like the cartoon of a fresco. She clenched her mouth firmly shut. He sat back down on the bed and took her hand . He stroked her hair. His voice was gentle suddenly. He traced a bar of the double wedding ring with her finger.

"Tell me what happened, sweetheart."

It was the gentleness that broached the wall. Her clenched jaws opened. She began to sob.

"He raped me."

Jimmy's hand stopped stroking.

"Hugh raped me."

"Son of a bitch!"

He leaped from the bed again. The bed rocked from his rage. She had seen this rage only once before when a coal company had bulldozed a house, laughing at the court order he waved at them. They waved another back at him. Hired guns. They wore them on their hips like old time gunslingers. Jimmy had gone and bought his own gun. You needed one in coal country, he told her, buying her the lady's special at the same time. You couldn't always depend on the law.

"Son of a bitch!" he yelled again, and headed toward the door.

"Where are you going?" She leaped up so suddenly she felt a wave of dizziness. She felt a jabbing pain in her knees as she cut in front of him, blocking the door.

"To find the son of a bitch.."

"No," she yelled. He looked at her and she knew suddenly he could knock her down if she stood in his way.

"What's going on here?" Sister was angry, herself. "What are you doing out of bed?" Linda felt herself pushed back to the bed. Sister turned to Jimmy, her eyes as stern as Mamaw's Christ. "I told you she wasn't well enough for any kind of upset." There weren't many men Sister admired. Jimmy was one of them. Her words had a immediate quieting effect.

"Don't let him go," Linda said. She knew his gun was in the truck. He'd kill him. And for a second she didn't know who would kill who? She just didn't want him to go.

"Nobody's going anywhere. Jimmy, sit down. And you lie back down and be quiet."

They both obeyed her. Exhausted.

"Did she tell you what happened?" He looked confused—as if he didn't know what to do without his rage.

"She didn't tell us anything. And we didn't ask. She wasn't in any condition to answer questions."

"You should have asked. He raped her. Hugh." Some of Jimmy's rage had come back. He sprung up again. "We can't let any more time go by. It's already Tuesday. We have to file charges."

"Sit down," Sister said again, and he did. Her voice was calm, but even she looked upset.

"Charges?" Linda was horrified even as one part of her was relieved that he was talking like a lawyer again. "I don't want to file charges." Did he know what filing charges would do?

"What are you talking about? The bastard raped you." He was shouting again, but quieted with one look from Sister.

"I don't want anybody else to know." Linda cringed at the thought. She hadn't wanted even them to know.

"You need to sleep," Sister ordered, the nurse again, and Linda did, suddenly, though she'd been sleeping for over a day. She needed to sleep again.

"Don't let Jimmy go," she begged. "Jimmy, don't go," she called out.

"He's not going anyway, are you, Jimmy. Jimmy?" And Linda wouldn't lie back down until she heard his voice assenting. "I'll stay." But he didn't come to the bed. He sat in a chair by the door. "I'll stay," he said again and she lay back down.

It was already dusk when she opened her eyes. She felt like each time she closed her eyes, she had lost another day. "Jimmy?" she asked.

"I'm here." He hadn't moved from his chair, a Shaker chair that made him sit straight, like an alert student. It couldn't be comfortable, she thought. "She's awake," he called through the door.

Caroline brought in more broth. Jeanette and Sister followed. "We're going to float away all your troubles with chicken broth, you being such a disappointment with the ham." Even Caroline had a hard time smiling at her joke. No one else tried. Linda looked at Jeanette in surprise.

"We called Jeanette," Sister told her. She had the no nonsense look she put on when she was cleaning up a mess. Part of the mess was her fault, her look indicated, but placing blame was beside the point. "Jimmy's right. We should have brought you to that hospital, death trap that it is. Should have found out sooner what happened. We're not making good decisions. We need another head."

"It's my fault," were the first words Jeannette said to her. "I could see trouble coming. Anybody could see trouble coming. I should have said something. I should have stopped it."

Her words were fresh tears at the wound. Anybody could see trouble coming. Anybody but her.

"I was so mad at you for bringing Kerry and putting us through that dinner. Then when I saw you with Hugh, I meant to caution you some but I thought, well, she knows what she's doing with these friends of hers." Jeanette shook her head, disgusted with herself. "Now don't take more meaning than I meant," Jeanette continued, catching herself up some. "I just meant you'd both been tipping the bourbon and the roads…" She stopped. She wasn't making things better.

Nobody said anything for awhile. Caroline finally started.

"Jimmy wants to file charges. We thought maybe you'd give us some advice on that."

"Charges?" Jeannette looked dubious.

"I don't want any charges," Linda said, and she saw Jimmy move restlessly with her words. Sister whispered something to him.

"She's right." Jimmy kept his eyes on Jeanette. "What good would charges do? Anybody see him rape her?'

The word was like a blow and they all flinched.

"Anybody can see he beat her up and we can charge him with that," said Caroline.

"He didn't beat me up." They all looked at her. Even Jimmy.

"We need to hear the whole story." Jeannette decided to take charge. "From beginning to end."

They were quiet as she told the story. It didn't take her long. Jeannette had gotten a pad and jotted down some notes as she spoke but didn't interrupt her. Linda could feel Jimmy as she spoke but he kept silent, too. It had gotten dark so quickly. She wondered what day it was. Caroline switched on the reading lamp by the bed, its soft glow framing Linda as she told her story—like an actress in front of the curtain, telling her lines directly to the audience.

"I need to ask you some questions, honey," Jeannette said quietly as she finished. "That OK?" Linda nodded.

"Are you interested in Hugh?" Jeanette was casual as she asked the question but it froze the rest of them in place like a tableau. Linda felt as if Jeanette had slapped her.

"As a student. I'm a teacher. That's why I invited him." She hated that her voice trembled. She hated Jeanette. Jeanette looked down and was quiet for a few seconds.

"He interested in you?"

Linda remembered the winks, the smiles. She looked at the wall again. Her cartoon face looked back. "A lot of men are interested," and knew that was beside the point. What had she told one boy? My face is up here? As if she could handle anything. Of course Hugh had been interested.

Jeanette waited again. "He's a good looking boy. I noticed him down at the housing hearing."

"I told him no, I fought him. I hit him in the nose. He bled all over. All over me." Her voice wasn't trembling now. It was angry. Sister looked ready to stop it. Jeannette shook her head at her.

"Of course you fought him, honey. Being attracted is no call to rape. I couldn't walk down the street if it was. We just have to know these things. It's all that bourbon. I've never seen that much bourbon, especially at Easter dinner. You'd think they'd have more sense."

"I asked them to bring it," Linda said.

Jeanette was speechless.

"It's hopeless, isn't it?" Jimmy said.

The record of her stupidity, Linda thought. Not ordinary dumbness, as Caroline would put it, but stupidity. Willful stupidity. Arrogance, self-deceit. She wasn't angry at Jeannette anymore.

"He raped her." Jimmy was on his feet again. "All the rest of that's not worth shit." He turned to Sister when he said this. She was the one keeping him in the room. She looked back at him calmly.

"You gonna' shoot him, Jimmy?" Sister wasn't one to keep things hidden. "That's what they do around here. I thought that since you were a lawyer, you might let the law try its hand."

"You heard. The law's not going to do anything." Jimmy looked like he wanted to pace but the crowded room kept him in his place.

"It may or may not. We haven't given it much of a chance." Sister put a hand on Jimmy's arm. Linda saw him tremble at the touch.

"She won't even press charges."

Sister looked at Linda. There was no more retreat—not the wall—not the swirl of the quilt—not the homey sweet sun on the ceiling. Sister looked at Linda and made her look back. "Worse things than losing. One of them is losing without putting up a fight." She bent over to retrieve the soup bowl by Linda's bed. She held it in one hand. With the other, she took a hand of Linda's. Holding hands with Sister felt very strange and very normal. "What happens if you don't press charges?" she continued. "Then I guess it's just your fault. That's what you think. Bad judgement. Or too much bourbon. Maybe you didn't use good judgement. I don't always use it myself. I didn't use when you showed up at the door. Thought I knew more than I did." She put the bowl down on the table and sandwiched Linda's hands in hers. "But the rape's not your fault. You fought him. Inviting him, the bourbon, that's not rape. There's worse things than losing."

Sister didn't say it all, didn't say she'd have to fight or Jimmy would. Jimmy might still fight. They were waiting for her. She wanted to sleep again. Wanted to close her eyes and wake up in a different place. But Sister held her eyes, held her hand. Linda's voice was a whisper but they all heard her.

"File the charges"

She looked at Jimmy looking at her again, trying to figure her out, sorting out her and Hugh. His attraction. Hers. Going off alone with him. Drinking with him. She saw Jimmy looking at her. "Jimmy," she called, and the old habit of her voice was too much for him.

He smiled a very small smile at her though he didn't come any nearer. "It's going to be alright, sweetheart," he said, "it's going to be all right."

She smiled back. "I know," she returned his lie, "I know."

Chapter 18

Rumors in the narrow river valley appeared as mysteriously as the morning fog that ringed the mountains and drifted down the hollows. Sometimes people knew things and didn't know how they knew them. Had someone told them? Most people were fair minded. They knew that the pretty young schoolteacher would have needed to be as cloistered as a nun to keep the gossip controlled. Even cloistering probably wouldn't have worked. People knew Linda had left the Easter party with Hugh. Drinking. Drunk. A teacher. This was common news by Monday afternoon. All day people waited for one of the two to show, but neither did.

Hugh came Tuesday but he had nothing to say. Others said it for him.

Hugh never said much of anything to anyone. Speaking up in Linda's class had been the exception. Since the Navy his old friends had drifted away. He had changed, people said, in that tone that meant changed for the worse. "Hugh ain't the same," one boy said. "Thinks too much."

Mamaw carried on about that. Not the thinking. But the being alone. She didn't think it right for him to stay home with her so much.

"You think I should go drinking with the boys more, Mamaw?"

"I hope to goodness that ain't all you can think of doing. If it is, I got plenty of chores around here I can think of." She worried him so much he'd been glad to tell her of the invitation to the Easter dinner. She'd been pleased. Rumors didn't make their way up the valley to Mamaw but she knew of the schoolteacher, had heard of her from Hugh and others. Knew she was pretty. Had heard enough of the young schoolteacher to have hopes that she might be the one to get the boy moving, get the boy out of himself. Mamaw didn't care that she was a foreigner. She wasn't prejudiced.

So she waited eagerly for some report of the party, for Hugh wasn't stingy with the little social life he had. Told her more than she wanted to hear most times. But he didn't tell her anything about Easter. She knew he'd brought someone home though how she knew that was hard to say. Nothing was out of place . But if he didn't want to talk about it, she wasn't going to press him. She felt a sadness. Figured the pretty young teacher had turned him down some way. She felt mad at the thought of anybody turning down her boy——of not seeing how much there was to him. She knew it was silly being mad—had heard there was a boyfriend, but still she felt a little peeved. Peeved at herself more than anything and how much stake she had been putting in a woman she hadn't even met. She listened to his silence and wanted to tell him there were others out there, others who would want him. But she wasn't going to press him.

Others pressed. "Needs two days to recover from you, Hugh," one boy jostled him in the lounge, and a group of them had laughed, but he didn't say anything. Didn't even grin. Just walked on by like they weren't there. Something about his silence made them back off. Something about his silence seemed dangerous. But the silence spread the rumors, multiplied them like smoke trails from different chimneys. Stories dribbled further out into the town. A fight of some sort. Hugh had beat his teacher up. Some kind of date gone bad. Her boyfriend, that radical lawyer, had beat her up, mad about the date. The men had squared off against each other up or were about to. There'd been threats. Guns. Bad blood. The men were spoiling for a showdown.

Kerry hadn't shown up Monday, either. A weak wisp of smoke connected Linda with that but it died like mist in the afternoon sun. Better knock before you walk in, students had teased each other when the office door was closed, but nobody really believed anything went on.

"Kerry and Linda?" A secretary scoffed. "Kerry and the bourbon bottle, you mean."

The rumors didn't upset the county. They involved foreigners mostly—except for Hugh and he was almost a foreigner anymore. And they were such wispy rumors—an afternoon's entertainment. People looked forward to the next tidbit of news, mildly grateful for the diversion from routine. People from the town began to have business at the college, hoping to catch a glimpse of Linda when she returned, speculating about how she'd carry herself. The torrent of rumor was like a flooded mountain stream that didn't subside until it had flooded every hollow. Then the people began to choose sides. They remembered, most of them, that Hugh was one of them, made strange by the navy, maybe, but one of their own still. Half the county related to him. And they remembered that the schoolteacher wasn't.

By five o'clock Tuesday, Hugh was one of a few people left in the school. His last class had been over for hours, but he hadn't wanted to go home. Home was Mamaw not asking him anything, but listening to his silence. He hadn't gone to any of his classes. He had heard Kerry had taken over Linda's classes and he wondered vaguely how she was doing. He knew the rumors were flying though not many people dared approach him anymore. He sat in the library with an open book in front of him, but he wasn't looking at it. Finals were the next week but he didn't care about them. School was an answer that wasn't working. He was looking at the hill behind the library. Enough leaves had sprouted to form a dense wall of trees. He wished the woods went on forever, like the view from Pine Mountain, though he knew, better than Linda, that it was just a mini-forest, that it ended fifty yards in. Not real. Not much was real.

When he saw the two deputies stop at the librarian's desk, he knew what was up even before he saw her pointing him out. One of the deputies was a third cousin of his though he hadn't seen him since they both were boys. Mamaw was the deputy's great-aunt. Probably had a place waiting for him up on the hill. Hugh frowned, thinking of the hill.

"You Hugh Richie?"

Hugh nodded.

"We're cousins of some sort."

"Third." Hugh answered. "Same tin-rust hair."

The cousin looked embarrassed. "You need to come along with us."

Hugh didn't say anything

"Don't you want to know what for?" the other deputy asked. He was a short fellow, a Wolf county boy. Not a cousin.

Hugh turned to him slowly, like he had interrupted a personal conversation. "What for?" he asked.

"Somebody's charged you with rape. A Miss Linda Eliot," the little deputy read. "She's some kind of teacher here, I think."

Around him he heard the gasp of the few students left in the library. One girl backed against the wall as if she expected him to make a break for it. He glanced at her and her eyes widened. He turned back to the deputy, still not saying anything. The deputy was holding a pair of handcuffs.

"Put your hands behind your back."

His cousin brushed the handcuffs aside. "He's kin," he said and Hugh saw the little man flush. He wondered idly if they were going to get into it for the deputy held the cuffs out for a second. Finally, he shrugged and put them away. His cousin took him by his arm and they started to walk to the squad car. People had come out of nowhere. The halls were almost crowded. They walked through the crowd as if it was a tunnel with no one saying a word. Their feet clattered in the hallway. No one said a word but Hugh knew that the story was already racing across the county faster than a summer storm blew up a hollow, faster than his life falling off a cliff.

He wondered how long it would be before Mamaw heard the story. She didn't have a phone, but others in their hollow did. When they reached the car, the little deputy stretched his arm out to push his head down but then stopped when he remembered he had no cuffs. Banty cock, Hugh thought. She'd be working out back, fiddling with the garden. Fiddling is what he called it because she had done all she could at this stage. Still too early for the corn, for the potatoes, for tomatoes. She'd be wondering when he'd get home so she could get him to fiddle, too. She missed the bigger garden though she agreed it didn't make much sense anymore. Nothing made much sense anymore. She'd look up in a an hour or so and think about that porch. Start to get mad. She knew his schedule better than he did. He'd have to tackle it soon or she'd be ripping it up herself, throwing her back out in the process. The meddling old woman. He shifted down as far as he could into the back seat of the cruiser so only the top of his head showed in the window. He saw people glancing as they passed, wondering who. His red hair narrowed the field of possibilities. That's how Mamaw got him to do half the chores he did, by threatening to do them herself. Telling Mamaw to take it easy was like telling her to die. She didn't take it easy. She had never taken it easy.

His cousin and the little deputy flanked him as he walked into the police station. They waited while the cop ahead of them processed two old men, so drunk they leaned against each other for support. He wondered how she would take this news. He hoped it wouldn't get to her for an hour or two until after the sun had set. She'd be hopping by then , a little worried, waiting supper for him and vowing he was going to eat it, cold or not. That'd be the best time to tell her. If there was a best time. He began to think of what he could tell her. It was the only thing he was worrying about as he lay on the bare cot and stared at the bare ceiling of the cell. What was he going to tell Mamaw about all this?

Chapter 19

Hugh spent only Tuesday night and Wednesday in jail. That night another of his cousins, a first cousin on his Mamma's side, put up some land for bail. Bail hadn't been set very high. He admitted having sex with Linda, but not rape. His story matched hers, "up to the point of penetration," as the sheriff put it. He was apologetic to Hugh. "We had to arrest you, boy. But that don't mean we have to keep you."

Linda returned to school on Thursday. No one expected her. She heard Hugh was out. She taught her classes. No one filled the chair Hugh usually sat in, front and middle. She looked around it as if he were still in it. The whole class acted as if he were still in it. Once her eyes wandered there and she blushed as if he'd caught her with a wink. He was the only one absent. All her classes were filled. The students sat up straight and watched her with more attention than they had given her all year. She stuck to the text and tried to involve them. But their answers were so wooden, she gave it up finally. Work on your own or in groups, she told them. I'll be here for questions. But they didn't have the nerve to ask the questions they longed to ask or the courage to discuss her with her sitting there. So the silence stretched through the days.

The silence stretched to her colleagues, too. Nobody mentioned to her what everybody talked about when she wasn't there. She wondered if Hugh was going through the same silence, the people staring, the unspoken words hovering behind their stares. How odd to think that they should be joined like this. They'd always be joined, at least in the county. Student and teacher, rapist and raped. She'd always be that schoolteacher.

She wasn't completely isolated. Tom Black, the history teacher, boomed his sympathy across the hall when he saw her. He scattered everyone else in the hallway as if they'd been pigeons set to by a Tomcat. But Linda didn't scatter. She was grateful, even for the booming. No secrets here, his booming said, none you be ashamed of. And she was comforted. And one of the secretaries, also, surprised her, a woman who hadn't said two words to her all year. "You hang in there, honey. Some of us know what you're going through."

But mostly, people left her alone as if it were the only kind thing to do. The first day back she surprised Kerry loading books into a box.

"You back already, honey?"

"Moving out?"

He kept his head down. "That little space across from the library finally got cleared out. Ain't much, but I thought you'd appreciate a little peace and quiet."

The space had been clear for months. She nodded.

"Your friends not too upset with me over that dinner, are they? Hoo boy. You'd think an ol' Kentucky boy like me would be on friendlier terms with the home stuff."

She couldn't think what he was talking about for a second. Oh, the dinner. "You'd think," she answered. She left him to finish moving. When she returned, Kerry was gone but LeeAnne, his wife, was waiting for her.

"I'm sorry about this," she said, pointing to Kerry's empty half of the office. "I told Kerry it was just a chicken shit thing ..." she stopped. "You just hang in there, honey."

Two hang in there, honeys, and Tom Black's booming voice. It could be worse, she thought.

Linda knew who she was before she had said a word. The school had emptied out for the summer. Final grades had been due the two weeks before, but she'd been granted an extension. Still, the secretary responsible for posting the marks had been gently pressing her all morning. She was trying to focus, but she hadn't even finished marking the last set of essays. Her mind kept wandering. She didn't even have the excuse of interruption, for no one but the secretary had disturbed her for hours. She rubbed her calf muscle. She had pulled it at the food pantry. Sister had her out there almost daily since school had ended— or since classes had ended. School wouldn't end until she got those grades in.

She was shorter than Linda had imagined and thinner, too. But she was still an imposing looking woman. She stood there, solid in the doorway, and they looked at each other for a moment or two.

"You Miz Eliot?"

She nodded.

"I'm Miz Richie, Hugh's grandmother."

"I know," she said, "I recognize you from his portrait."

"Portrait?" She looked puzzled for a second. "Oh, you mean that writing he done. He showed me that. I don't know I'm anything like he wrote, but I never much thought I looked like my photographs, either. It's hard for a body to see hisself like others see him. Can I close this here door?"

Linda pulled Kerry's chair over and locked the door. She was busy noticing the details Hugh hadn't described, the hair cropped short and simple but somehow as elegant as any salon cut; the clear blue eyes, sad now, innocent, but intelligent. The way she moved, quick and direct, with nothing of the old woman about her.

"I've wanted to meet you for a long time," she told her.

"I've wanted to meet you, too, ever since Hugh brung home that first writing. I thought when I read it that there's a teacher who can bring that boy home to hisself. I didn't expect to be meeting you like this, though. I guess you didn't either."

They sat silent for a few moments. Linda realized that somehow she had been expecting this visit. She wondered if Mamaw, she thought of her as Mamaw, would ask her to drop the charges. She didn't know what she'd do if she did.

"I've come to ask you to forgive him." She said it direct.

"Forgive him?"

"He's done a terrible thing. He knows it. He should be here hisself, but that ain't possible. So I'm here for him. Can you forgive him?"

"He told you the truth?"

"I asked him and he told me. He might lie to the whole world but he ain't gonna lie to me. He told me how you came up to see the land and the graveyard. I knowed somebody been there when I came home next day, but he never told me who. Not till it all came out. He says he never meant for it to happen, not that way. He didn't plan on it. He wants you to know that, too."

Didn't plan on it. She wanted to believe that. It had made it worse, the idea that all along ... "I don't think," she faltered some, "I don't ... know if I can drop the charges."

Mamaw shook her head. "Of course, you don't know. But nobody's asking you to drop no charges. Hugh telling me the truth ain't him telling the world. I can't tell them. Wouldn't do no good anyway, and I can't put my own grandboy in jail. He goes to jail, it's his own doing."

She breathed heavily as if the speech had winded her. She looked very tired, but took a deep breath and continued. "What he's asking you is to forgive him. In your heart. Forgive him. I don't know that I could. Probably not. I ain't the forgiving type. You forgive him. Then the Lord. Then himself."

"What about you?"

"He didn't rape me." Mamaw didn't flinch from the word. "Nor the Lord. Your forgiveness comes first."

"It was my fault," Linda said suddenly. "My fault. My stupidity."

Mamaw shook her head. "Your fault? You asked him to rape you? What he told me is that you tried to fight him off every way you could. Almost broke his nose. That don't sound like it was your fault."

"But I should have known better. Everybody says I should have known better."

For the first time, Mamaw looked more mad than sad.

"What everybody says usually ain't worth much. Should have knowed what? Hugh's a good boy. That's what you knowed, and a good boy don't go around raping women just 'cause he's got the opportunity. It don't matter how much whiskey he's drunk or how much whiskey she's drunk. Hugh's a good boy who's done a terrible thing—a thing he's gonna pay for most all his life. But that ain't your fault. It ain't my fault, either. It's his fault."

Hugh was a good boy. She realized as she heard the words that she'd been mourning that, mourning the lost idea of Hugh's goodness almost as much as she'd been mourning her disgrace, mourning even as she felt herself a fool for having believed in him, mourning everything she had thought and known about him. But if he was a good boy, a good man, if she had seen this and knew this, then it wasn't her fault. She'd been right to trust him.

But it didn't make sense.

"How could a good boy do something like that?"

Mamaw sighed, her anger gone as quickly as a summer squall. "I don't know, honey. I just know it's so. I've seen a whole lot of bad done by good people. I've done bad myself, and I'm a good person. Did a whole lot of bad thinking I was doing good. I throwed out Hugh's daddy 'cause I wouldn't allow no drinking. Everybody told me I done the right thing, but I knew it weren't so. I didn't make him a drunk but I didn't help none, either. I was hard, too hard. And proud of it, too.

"It was hardness that made me stop speaking to my brother Fred. You know him from the writing Hugh did. I had cause again. I've always had cause for what I did, it made it easier to call it right, but it weren't right. And I knowed it, and it's caused a whole lot of pain. Right to this day. His children and his children's children never felt welcome on the land their own people settled. Never felt no reason to try and stop people from destroying it. Now they're tearing the land apart, right up to the graveyard, and they might get the graveyard yet. I'm fighting them, and I'm gonna fight them till I'm in the graveyard myself, but I know they couldn't have gotten the land if the people hadn't been torn apart themselves. And I know that part of that is my doing.

"But I was a hard woman, hard to talk to, hard when it came to forgiveness. You want to know how a good boy could do what he did? There was a time once when I'd say it weren't possible. No good boy could do that. Now I'm asking you to forgive something I never would have forgave, something I couldn't imagine forgiving. But I know he don't have a chance if you don't forgive him, and it's Providence's judgement on my own hardness that I'm the one asking. I'm asking you to be an old woman, to see what it took me a lifetime to see."

They sat for awhile. Their silence didn't seem to bother either of them.

"You know, when Hugh was a little boy, he talked more than three other children put together. I told him I had eleven children in that house one time, but he had more questions in a week than all those other children had in a year. A whole lot more questions than I had answers. Now I keep asking myself, how that little boy growed up to do what he did? I said it was his doing, not mine, not yours, and it was, but I keep seeing that little boy, with the whole world promised in front of him."

She paused again, and for the first time, tears clouded her clear blue eyes. "He ain't got the whole world anymore. Right now he might be getting some jail time. But that ain't what's grieving me. What's grieving me is that he's in danger, mighty danger, of losing that little boy. He's caught between selves. He's been caught a long time. I thought you encouraging him might push him in the right direction. And it did, for awhile. And maybe that scared him. Maybe he seen what he could be and it scared him so he had to tear it down—had to get back to the bottom where his daddy ended, and his Mamma's headed, where nobody expects nothing from you. Especially yourself. There's a whole passel of folks around here that nobody expects nothing from. And that's what they give out, too. It ain't your fault you showed him something else. And nobody'd blame you if you gave up on him now. You have cause, more than cause."

She got up then. "I've taken up a whole lot of your time. I know it must be a busy time for you." She looked out the window. "That's a pretty view you got here. I remember this land fifty years ago. It belonged to kin of my Mamma's. Used to be a creek run right near here, I think."

"It comes back when it rains," Linda said.

"I guess it does. Covering up and drying out a creek are two different things. It broke my heart when they stripped this land. But it's looking pretty now. Not like it was, but things come back, one way or the other."

Linda put her hand out to shake. Mamaw looked at it a second, then reached out to embrace her. Mamaw's body was a mixture of hard and soft. Linda felt herself pressed into Richie flesh again and the shock of it was like a dip into a cold stream. As quickly as she had grabbed her, Mamaw let her go and stood back, looking at her face.

"You do what you can, honey. That's all anybody can ask. If you can forgive him, you send word any way you want. If you can't, he's gonna have to live with that, too. We live with what we have to, what we've brought on ourselves and what's brought on us by others. Sometimes it seems like the past wants to bury us before our time, that we can't see what's coming by being blinded by what's been. I can't put him in jail, but what I can do I will. People will know I came visiting. People will know you're a good woman. They'll hear me tell it and it might do some good. I hope so."

She rummaged around in the giant bag she carried.

"Here's something Hugh told me to give you. I told him I'd see how it went before I'd give it to you. I don't know what's in it. I didn't have the heart to read it and maybe you don't, either. He says it's the last paper you gave them to do. He says it's up to you what you want to do with it. It's all there. He says he knew even when he was lying he was gonna have to tell you the truth. Just like he told me the truth. 'Cause you told the truth. He says he didn't have any choice once you done that. 'Cause you had more to lose than he did. He told me to thank you for that."

She paused at the doorway.

"I thank you for it, too."

Chapter 20

Mamaw's visit was soon known and Linda felt the shift. A few more people asking how she was holding up. A few more smiles. But most people didn't rush to change their opinion. Opinions in most people cleaved like Krazy glue. It'd take more than one old woman, even if she was Hugh's grandma, to unstick what they knew. They just wondered what was wrong with Mamaw. Old woman so rattled she didn't know what she was doing. And they blamed that on Linda, too.

The drinking, especially, went down hard. People sometimes spoke of Hugh as if he had been a boy of fifteen or so rather than a man of twenty-five. She got that boy drunk, they said, and then cried foul when he did what only you'd expect, like egging a dog on to chase the chickens, just for fun, and then blaming the dog for going too far.

A lot of people just didn't care what the facts were.

"All this fuss just because a young woman doesn't have the sense God gave a turkey," is how one person put it.

"Will things ever get back to normal?" she asked Jeannette. They were back at the food pantry. Sister had come by and redrafted her.

"Time to feed the hungry," is all Sister said.

Linda tugged at a fifty-pound bag of beans. The ache in her muscles felt good.

Jeanette paused to stretch her back, groaning a little. She had more than once grumbled that morning about "tyrant nuns" and how you'd think the way Sister issued orders that there had never been a Reformation. "Depends on what you call normal, I suppose. Things will get better."

Better. They were better already though sometimes the memories and sometimes the pain lay in her bones like a heavy sedative so that she could barely move. But times like that were rarer. When she came back to her pain after forgetting it for an hour, for a morning, she felt vaguely disloyal, as if she had betrayed the pain, trivialized it by forgetting it even for awhile.

The pain came back when she saw Jimmy. He had come to pick her up and helped her carry the last cases of food from the truck to the edge of the platform. They smiled at each other like polite strangers. Things weren't getting better with Jimmy. He didn't disappear like Kerry. He came to see her every day. He was going to stick by her. She could feel the resolve in him, could see it in his eyes. But something was missing. Lost. She didn't want resolve. They had secrets now—both of them. They hadn't before. Not like this. Hugh was a name they never mentioned, but it hung in the air. She was afraid. Afraid of what he was thinking. Afraid of what he was planning. Hard decisions needed to be made. And she wasn't ready for them.

"Jimmy," she said to him when they got home and they were sitting on the small porch of her A-frame. He liked to sit outside lately and wouldn't often come in, even for a drink. "Jimmy, don't you want to make love?"

He looked up surprised. The trees were in full summer bloom and made the A-frame seem a little island in the forest. She had never asked the question before. She had never had to. He paused before he answered and the pause was like a rip in her lungs—as if she'd been sprinting uphill.

"I don't know what I want," he answered. "I don't know," and he looked as if he wanted to sprint himself. Go on, she thought. Run. Run.

Jimmy watched her as she hunched her shoulders together. She had taken to wearing large sweatshirts again, shapeless. If she meant to hide, it wasn't working. The suggestion of breasts behind the large shirts was sexier than a tight sweater could ever have been. At least to him. She insisted the shirts kept her cool, like a Bedouin's robes. It's not that, he wanted to tell her, but knew she wouldn't believe him. How could he not want to make love to her—here, now— but he couldn't. He still saw Hugh, but it wasn't that. It wasn't jealousy. It wasn't even her wanting another man, going off alone with another man, though he had not wanted another woman since he met her. Not really wanted.

Every woman he glanced at, admired, just reminded him of how much he wanted Linda. Wanting Linda was a hunger that stayed with him always. Linda, Linda, he longed to call her back though she sat three feet from him and wanted him to want her. And he did. But he couldn't.

He came up every day and sat by her. In his mind he held her, caressed her. It wasn't that another man had entered her, raped her, raped him. He could come back from that. He could heal. She could heal. It wasn't that.

He couldn't grip it. He didn't know how to grip it. All his life he had grappled with people, gone in close and left them hurting. Leave the bully bleeding, his dad would tell him. Don't worry about being beat up. Everybody gets beat up, but make the bully think twice, think three times before he tackles you again. Leave the bully hurting. He fought the bullies everywhere. He fought them in Philly. He fought them here. It didn't matter if he lost. Hurt the bully. Get in close. Grip him, grab him by the balls.

But he couldn't grip anymore. He'd leave her most afternoons—go driving, wandering. He didn't go back to his briefs. He got deferrals, did the minimum. Did less than the minimum. But no one pressed him. Even judges gave him all the time he wanted. He didn't want time. He had too much time. He'd drive by his client's broken house and find them harvesting lettuce and early potatoes. They'd offer him their fruits but he declined. What would he do with them? They had heard about Linda and were patient with him. Kind. But their eyes held the question and he didn't know the answer anymore. Didn't know if they shouldn't take the five thousand. What more could he do for them. What could he do for anyone? What kind of man was he? The question lay in the shape of the wife's back as she turned away from him and continued hoeing. Why would you fight for us if you don't fight for yourself?

And he wanted to fight. It would be easy to fight. He'd sit on a dark mountain road and aim the gun at his windshield, a World War II relic, a Smith and Wesson .45 revolver his father had brought back and stored away for thirty five years with the rest of the war's mementos. He had gone and collected it, registered it in his name, oiled it and polished it and stuck it in his truck and thought about it as much as his father had those thirty five years. Until now. He'd hold the gun and look down its long slim barrel, grip it till his arm began to ache and the grip felt real, felt whole. But his grip would slip finally, slide from the handle. And he'd look at the gun and wonder. Once he aimed the gun at a tree thirty or so feet away, a slim young walnut tree pushing its way up between two maples. He fired at it once and the sound made him jump as if it were unexpected, a surprise. As if someone had come from behind and fired just to see him startle. The bullet split the young walnut. He wondered if it would survive the split, grow a bark lump over the wound.

He drove around but never looked for Hugh except for the time he left jail. He knew he was in town, knew he had moved down from the mountain to live with his uncle, once saw him strolling toward the town library. Free. Easy. Proud. But he never looked for him. He felt the gun in his pocket when he saw him but he let him go by.

He sat in bars—scruffy redneck bars where no one—except a stray client—would know him. He sat in the corners— out of the way— and no one noticed him. No one noticed the gun bulging in his inside jacket, or thought twice about him wearing a jacket in the Kentucky heat. It wouldn't have mattered if they had noticed. Other men wore jackets. He tried to drink. But it did nothing for him. Some kind of Irishman, he thought. Can't even drink. Don't even want to. He'd stare at his glass till the bartender started making noises about filling up space. Then he'd gulp the drink and order another one to stare at. Or he'd give up the effort and leave.

He was giving up the effort one night in a bar on Main Street when Hugh walked in. The bar was crowded, but the men made way for Hugh, shouting and hollering. The case was a favorite subject at the bars in town and they'd been waiting for him to show up.

"So how was she, boy?" an older man started. " She gonna' give you an A or just a pass?" The crowd of men roared out their laughter.

"He ain't got no A. Too sloppy ," another shouted. "Gonna' have to do it over." Jimmy watched Hugh as the crowd laughed and whooped around him. Hugh gave them a small smile when he entered the bar, but hadn't said anything yet.

"His grade ain't the question," the bartender put in. He was a young man—not much older than Hugh. "She gave his grade to the sheriff.

She just don't want to fail you. She wants to jail you. What I want to know is what kind of grade you giving her?" And the crowd joined in.

"A+ for tits!"

"D+ for tits you mean," the bartender said, and the crowd laughed harder when they got it.

"Come on, boy," the old man finally said when they had quieted down some. "You college boys got the life. What grade you giving her?"

Jimmy had joined the edge of the crowd off to Hugh's side. He waited for Hugh's grade. He felt calm for the first time in months. Hugh was looking down at his drink .

"Shit, you gotta' give her a C," the bartender broke in again. " I'd give ol' lady Jenkins a C." The town had given her a 100th birthday party the week before. But still Hugh didn't answer. The men began to squirm. They'd been friendly before though the old man's "college boys" had the beginning of an edge.

Hugh finally looked up. "Can't talk about it , fellas. Lawyer says I can't talk about it," as if they'd been asking him to share legal strategy.

"Shit, boy," the old man was disgusted and turned away. Others drifted away also till Hugh was left alone with his drink. He looked at it but didn't lift it up. A fellow drinker, Jimmy thought.

Jimmy felt his grip relax. He walked past Hugh and paused outside the bar. He needed air. He gulped it in like gulps of water. He stood there panting. He took his hand out of his pocket and started to flex his fingers. He could feel the blood returning to his arm, traveling up his shoulder, into his brain. His calm had disappeared again but so had something else. He felt like he was waking up.

He didn't know how he long he stood there, but when he looked up, Hugh was leaving the bar and they caught each other's eyes. They stared at each other and Jimmy tried to read Hugh's expression. It wasn't what he expected. Not cocky. Not fearful. Friendly. It didn't make sense. As if he liked him. As if they were old friends and he was glad to see him there. They didn't speak. Hugh stood there as if he were waiting for something. Jimmy didn't know what. Finally, Hugh nodded to him and turned away.

Hugh had spotted Jimmy when he and his cousin were slipping out the back door of the jail. He figured Jimmy meant to be spotted. He had put himself five feet away and looked like he'd been there awhile. He would have taken clients through the same door, Hugh realized. Hugh wondered if Jimmy was going to shoot him down right there. For some reason, he remembered the gun control argument in class. What'd he say? Born in the wrong family, drink at the wrong bar. Which was this? He hoped his cousin would get his bail back.

"Who the hell's that?" his cousin asked.

"The boyfriend," Hugh answered and the cousin looked puzzled for a second and then connected.

"Hoo boy. I think I'd be carrying from now on if I was you."

"I reckon so."

The cousin dropped him off at Uncle Billy's. Mamaw had been down to see him in the jail, but he couldn't see living with her for awhile. She wouldn't press him. He knew her style. Except her not saying anything was pressing—her not nagging him or fussing at him was a different kind of pressure. At Uncle Billy's everybody welcomed him home like a veteran. Like he'd been to the wars. Nobody had greeted him like this when he came home from the navy. Folks hardly noticed. But now friends and relations dropped in all the time. Even his mamma showed up, dragging her latest boyfriend behind her. She still looked good to Hugh but the quality of her men was declining. She talked about trashy women. She had warned Hugh before about them.

"She's not trashy, Mamma."

She shook her head. He was just too nice. Always been his trouble.

Hugh half expected daddy to show up, too, but he guessed he was down too deep a well for even Hugh's news to reach him. Hugh felt like he was in his own well. People's voices echoed around him. He'd almost wished the VA money wasn't still coming in so he'd have to get work. He had too much time. He couldn't go back to the college. Not for awhile. He heard Linda had. Folks let him know everything about Linda. He was certain folks told her about him. Like they were married. Like they'd want to know everything about each other. He admired her going back to school. Brave of her. Linda. He lay on the couch in his uncle's living room and thought of her. Thought of that night. Linda.

He half wished his cousin had left him in jail. Time wasn't your own in jail. You just passed it. Served it. You didn't have to fill it—didn't have to get through it. He wandered around town, half expecting to see Jimmy again. He thought he saw him once but when he turned he was gone.

He'd been a week out of jail before he dropped by the bar on Main Street. Your odds of getting shot in there were as good as any in the county. He'd hoped to slip in quietly and nurse a beer but it was like the crowd was waiting for him. They greeted him like he'd just won the game. Men reached out to touch him, slapped him on the back, on the ass. He was one of theirs. They set him up with a drink. He heard the jokes about the grades and the tits. Their laughter crowded him. He tried to join in but he couldn't manage more than a small smile. And then not that. The crowd grew quiet and he realized they were asking him something. They wanted details. An old man was looking at him. A hard drinking old man who looked like one strong cough would take him off. Daddy probably looked like that if he looked that good. The old man was saying something about college boys. The bartender was joining in. They were waiting for him.

He mumbled something about lawyers and they drifted away. "Shit, boy" the old man said and looked pure disgusted. He didn't want the drink anymore. Couldn't follow daddy down that well. Had to find another one all his own.

Jimmy was an old friend waiting when he walked out. He wondered if he'd been in the bar. This it? They stood five feet apart and suddenly Hugh felt good. He looked at Jimmy and liked him. Liked him. He stood there waiting but Jimmy just stared back. Not tonight, he guessed. He nodded and walked away.

He moved back to Mamaw's the next day. She greeted him with a look and he answered her questions. She didn't have many. She left him alone for a couple of days, watching him as he wrote. They ate in silence but it wasn't a bad silence. It was OK. After two days he gave her a package.

"You gonna' see Linda. Miz Eliot." It was a statement.

She nodded.

"Give her that. Tell her I'm sorry. Not worth much but I am. Tell her I never planned anything. That's important."

Mamaw just waited.

"You tell her it's not her fault. None of it. People'll tell her different but you remind her. It's all in there," he pointed to the package. "She can do with it what she wants. It's up to her."

He heard Mamaw pulling at the new lumber on the porch before she left.

"Boy, are you gonna' tear this porch off before it falls in the creek or do I have to start ripping myself?"

Hugh walked over to the door. Ten years in that porch yet, he thought. "You got to keep a body busy, don't you, Mamaw?"

"Idle hands are the devil's workshop" is all she said as she climbed into the truck.

Chapter 21

For their final effort, she had asked her students to combine one or two of the modes. She had started out as a firm believer of the modes. She liked the way they structured thinking: classification, cause and effect, definition, comparison- contrast, process, etc. How orderly they were. But her students weren't orderly. Their thinking was sloppy, chaotic, if you could even call it thinking. She had spent endless hours trying to prod them into the modes, but they had been so resistant, so dense, like half-wild cattle, refusing to be corralled. She had reluctantly begun to suspect that they just weren't intelligent enough to understand. And lately, she was just worn out. She didn't have the energy to prod as much.

Without her prodding, they had begun to write better.

Hugh had decided to combine process, a how-to-essay with an extended definition. He entitled it: How to do your family proud.

You taught us way back when we first did definition essays, that it ain't no use in going on about something if you haven't "defined your terms sufficiently." I remember you pointing at us with your finger extended and kind of underlining those words. "Define your terms sufficiently." I thought the poor old boy ahead of me was going to pee in his pants when you pointed at him. You said we all have different meanings floating around in our heads, and that it's a wonder that we understand each other even half the time. Certain words were particularly tricky. They'd just kind of float off "into balloon heaven" if you didn't tie them down.

"Balloon heaven," that old boy ahead of me whispered. "What the hell is she talking about?"

I see right off that I'm going to have to tie down that word proud, or pride, or it's going to float right off out of sight. I looked it up in the big dictionary, the one they got sitting on its own table like a stone monument in the middle of the library. It ran on more than a page with different meanings. Just when I thought it had to run out, it came up with another. Kind of prideful, itself, I thought. I'd say that old dictionary seemed to have an "exaggerated self-esteem."

I've known lots of people with exaggerated self-esteem. There was a little guy in the Navy, couldn't have been more than five-six in high heels, used to have an exaggerated self-esteem of his own fighting ability. As many times as he got knocked down, he bounced right up. I wonder if that's pride or just plain stupidity? I never could decide. Of course, he done it himself—setting himself up to get knocked down. People might say that that's just plain dumb. He got what he deserved.

Getting what you deserve ain't supposed to get you no sympathy, but I always thought that getting what you deserved made the punishment worse. I mean the fellow who gets what he doesn't deserve at least has the comfort of knowing that, of being the victim, of sorts. But the other guy, he gets nothing.

One time, I saw that little guy pause a few seconds before he got up again. He just lay there, like a boxer taking the benefit of the count to rest up some, but I understood him to be considering whether or not to get up again at all, considering whether it was worth it or not, knowing it was a big guy he was fighting, a real big guy— it was me, in fact— knowing that he was just going to be knocked flat again. But he got up. I suppose that's a kind of pride, a kind of stupid pride, one that don't bear much thinking about, but pride.

A sense of one's own dignity or worth; self-respect is that dictionary's next meaning. What confuses me is how you know that that sense of one's own worth ain't exaggerated self-esteem. How that self-respect ain't just another hot air balloon, the kind you said would float off if we ain't careful.

Especially, if you're too smart to keep from knowing how dumb you are.

When I was knocking that little fellow down, and he kept bouncing back up like one of those dolls with the sand bottoms, I knew I had to keep knocking him down for my own self-respect. I couldn't let a little bitty guy like that topple me over. I'd have had every runt in the Navy beating on me. So I kept beating on him 'till I felt sick down to my stomach with every blow I landed, 'till every time I pulled my fist back, it was covered with blood. And I kept pounding, for my self-respect. For my pride, I guess.

Only when they finally took the little fellow away, I didn't feel much pride. I felt little and mean, like somebody had pricked my balloon. I never could figure that out, why something I did for my pride should have made me feel so unprideful, so to speak.

I guess I just didn't feel the "delight or satisfaction in achievement" the dictionary says I should feel when proud. I don't know that I ever felt much "delight" in achievement. Now Mamaw, when she's finished hoeing a row of corn and looks back, you can tell she's proud of what she's done. I look back at a row I've done, and I just see a row. I see the weeds that are coming and the weeds that are gone, but I don't see much delight. I feel my back aching but I don't feel much satisfaction. I guess I don't see much point in any of it.

"You see the point in eating, don't you?" Mamaw said one time when I had got mighty tired of hoeing. I must have been about fourteen or so and we'd been out in the field most of a week. It was some kind of spring vacation, not that I ever saw any vacation part of it. And the spring was more like summer. It just seemed like that field would never end.

"Well, of course I see the point in eating," I tell her. "But I don't see why we should go priding ourselves just 'cause we manage to put some food on the table."

Oh that made her as mad as a preacher with a backsliding congregation when I said that. She reared up at the end of that row, and I was glad to be a distance from her 'cause I had the feeling that that hoe she was waving about might have been bouncing off my head if I'd been nearer.

"There's a pride in just surviving," she shouted, and that shout raised a whole flock of crow birds from the trees, just setting there waiting for us to clear out so they could peck the seeds we had planted. "There's pride," Mamaw shouted, "just in getting through the day. In getting through life without doing anybody a major harm. There's pride in getting your crops raised, in raising your children, too. Pride in setting them on the right path."

"What for?" I asked. We were three, four rows apart and that encouraged my bravery some. "What good has it done you? All those kids you raised, half of them have gone down with the county. And the county's going down quick. You say yourself it don't raise half what it used to."

"It raises what it needs to. And that's all you can ask."

She didn't say anything about the children for awhile, and I was feeling kind of mean having said that in the first place. I knew she'd get around to commenting sooner or later, 'cause Mamaw's a bit like that little banty in the Navy, you could knock her down but you couldn't keep her down. As soon as she caught her breath, she'd be up and it didn't matter how bloody she was.

She finally stopped hoeing altogether and gave me her full attention.

"It ain't your doing or your fault if the crops you planted come up wrong. If the seed's right, and you weeded and you watered, if you did the things you needed to do and you did them in the right time, you did all you could. You got a right to be proud, then, even if everything turned out wrong. Even if you made the wrong decisions, if you planted corn when you should have planted potaters, and the corn goes bad, or the potaters get the blight, you did what you thought was best at the time, and the Lord don't ask anything more from you, and you don't need to ask anything more from yourself. You got a right to be proud then."

"So nothing's anybody's fault," I yelled back. I must have had my own dander up some 'cause I had learned early on you didn't sass back at Mamaw. Even with most of a field between us, it wasn't a safe thing to do. She'd been known to take off after a child or a man even and not stop till she caught him even if the catching took most of the day. But she weren't the only punching dummy in the family, I reckon, and fourteen's not the most tactful age.

"It is just the Lord's doing," I continued. "He's the reason why everything's crapped up. We can rest easy in the Lord."

I could see her considering whether to take off after me or not, those word "crapped up" especially not sitting right with her, or me mocking one of her favorite lines, the resting easy in the Lord, and I was considering myself when to start running, but she just took a deep breath and kept explaining.

"A whole lot ain't the Lord's doing. What we done and others are doing to the land ain't the Lord's doing. When my great-grand daddy wore out farms like there was an endless supply of them, that weren't the Lord's doing. When we tear up something good, like those fellows do who tear up the earth for coal, it ain't the Lord's doing. A whole bunch of it is our fault—that means your fault and that means my fault. That don't mean we can leave it at that. That'd be too easy. We gotta take the blame— and the shame, and we got to live with that shame and make that shame come out clean again. We got to keep on going even when we know we've been going wrong. But if we live with the shame and don't try to run away from it, and work with it, well, then the Lord says we can be proud again. The Lord don't expect people not to have shame. He don't expect no perfect people. He made angels to be perfect and even they didn't turn out all right. We just got to keep on trying, not laying it all on the Lord, not laying it all on ourselves."

She took a pause then and looked at me like she wanted to hoe me like she hoed that row. Every preacher we ever had said that if Mamaw'd been a man, she'd be the best preacher in Kentucky. I didn't think she had to be a man. Even at fourteen, even getting ready to sass her words back at her, I knew she had all the wisdom I'd ever need.

"I'll tell you one thing, though," she continued, "the Lord ain't going to feed us if we don't feed ourselves, and we ain't going to feed ourselves if we don't get back to work. The next time I see you I want to see your back bent like one of those question marks. That's what you are, just one big question mark, and I'm all out of answers for the present."

We went back to work then, Mamaw all sermoned out for the present. Work and trouble. I was the source of a whole lot of both. I don't suppose she ever did get much "delight in possessions of children" which is what that old dictionary has next, "a person or thing in which pride is taken as in 'his sons are his pride.'"

Her sons weren't usually much to be proud of, though most of them turned out better than my daddy. Daddy's pride was that he could drink most anybody under the table. After he got them there, he might join them or he might just lay down where he was. He weren't proud that way. My uncles and aunts mostly turned out better than daddy, but I don't see that they did all that well. They survived. Or most of them did. I had one uncle killed in a fight and one aunt who disappeared so we don't right know if she survived or not. Mamaw might think that's enough, but I still ain't sure that's such an achievement. Rocks survive, and mountains, though not all of them with these new coal stripping machines. Rats survive, too. They survive when just about all the other wild life's been stripped from these hills.

"That ain't surviving," Mamaw answered me when I point that out to her. It sounds like I spent my childhood arguing with her, and when I look back, I think I did. "When you lose the best of yourself forever and there's no retrieving it, you ain't survived."

"Well maybe that's where I am now, Mamaw." I was considerably older when I said that. It was just a few days ago, in fact.

She didn't answer me at first. I thought maybe I had finally wore her down, but I should have known better. She started talking about coal mines.

"You know, some of those old mines have been played out for fifty years. Nobody thought there was anything down in them worth retrieving. But with the new machines and new ways of doing things, they discovered there's a whole lot of good coal down there yet. They've just got to keep digging, got to keep hoping."

"A whole bunch of them mines ain't worth digging up, though," I answered. "All the best coal's been mined up long ago, it ain't worth the expense and the effort. All you get is a bunch of sulfur gas spoiling the water and fouling the air."

"You don't know that until you dig some. The easy coal's gone and now you got to work some," Mamaw said. "And a little sulfur smell ain't gonna to kill you. You always were particular about smells, like pigs were put on the earth just to plague you. But you like eating them. That's 'cause you know and I know that the mud they've been rolling in ain't of no account. All that filth can wash off with a good bristle brush. If it takes some skin, that don't much matter, either."

Well Mamaw can get your head spinning what with her talk of coal mines one moment and pigs the next, but I got her drift. I tell her she missed her calling and ought to have been a lawyer but she says she has her hands full just being what she is.

She's the best of what she is, I'll give her that, which is the dictionary's next definition: "the pick of a group, the flower—as in the pride of the Yankees." I don't know that she'd like being called the pride of the Yankees, but she's the pride of these hills.

Only what I don't understand is why things keep going down hill, from Mamaw to Daddy to me. Once Mamaw would have said that Daddy was just a dip in an upward progression, but I'd say he was more like the beginning of the slide to oblivion. Daddy never hurt nobody except himself. I wish I could say that, but you and I both know I can't. I like

Mamaw's image there of digging deep for the best coal, but the only thing I've been able to find digging deep has been a lot more dirt, a lot of gas that shouldn't be let in polite company, even letting it go alone by yourself smells up the place so you can hardly bear to live with yourself.

But Mamaw says I just have a finicky nose, that a bad smell ain't going to kill me, and that's there's lots of good meat under all that slime.

I'm going to have to take her word for that as someone who maybe knows better than I do, someone who's lived longer and borne more and kept coming back, kept surviving. And now she's going to have to survive what I done, and you are, too. And I'm sorry she's had this put on her. I never thought of her as old, but I know she is, and I know it's a hard thing I put on her.

Of course, she ain't the only one I put it on. She ain't even the first. Two people seemed like they thought there was good coal way down there, two people I seemed determined to prove wrong. One I thought I'd drag down in the dirt with me just to show her how wrong she was. I thought I might even keep her down there in the dirt for company. But she got back up and she says, you might cover me in dirt, but that don't mean I am dirt. Under all the filth you can lay on me, I'm still me. First chance I'll wash that dirt off. It ain't but skin deep.

Which is more than I can say. "Pigs got to be scalded," I said to Mamaw. That mud they've been rolling in so long has gotten deep under their skin. "They need to be dipped in boiling water to get clean."

"So you dip them," she says back. "If that's what you need to do."

"It ain't likely somebody survives that kind of dipping," I say.

"You'll survive," she says to me, "if you want to."

"Now that's just it," I says, "I don't know if I want to."

You know, one thing I said keeps coming back to me. I guess I didn't drink enough bourbon or I just have a powerful nagging memory. "I'm going to fuck me an English teacher," I said. Only I didn't fuck me no English teacher. I just rolled her in the dirt a little, but she got right back up. Now that's pride. Ain't no doubt about it.

I fucked me a good old boy. I fucked him good, and then I left him in the dirt. He ain't got back up yet. I don't know if I much want him to. Most people expect that's where he belongs. Except for Mamaw. Mamaw says he just has to make up his mind to take his scalding like the pig he's been. That there's good meat under all that muck. And he's willing to if he could see the point of it, the point of going on. Of surviving.

"Pride," Mamaw tells me again. "For the pride of it."

"What have I got to be proud of, Mamaw?"

"Not much yet," she says, for Mamaw ain't one to sugarcoat anything. She figures if the medicine don't make you shudder, it ain't going down right, or it ain't the right medicine. "But your life ain't over yet. Not if you don't want it to be. Only you got to set right what you can set right."

I told her I didn't know if I could set anything right, but that I'd try. I'd swallow what I always thought of as pride and what I see now was just that exaggerated self-concept, a big, good old boy blow hard. Worth no more than a high on bad liquor, and leaving me with a hangover I don't suppose will go away any time soon.

I'm sorry, Linda. I know I don't have much right to call you that anymore. I know we're not friends anymore. We ain't ever going to be friends anymore. Some things don't come back. But I don't hardly think of you as Miss Eliot. I haven't for a long time. I'm sorry, Linda, sorrier than you probably will ever know. They're going to tell you that a lot of what happened was your fault. It ain't so. Don't you believe them, Linda. It's just their way of bringing you down into the dirt with them. You got too much pride to stay down there, Linda. None of it was your fault.

None of it at all.

Well, that pride has proved some balloon and I guess I floated off with it for all my trying to tie it down. More like balloon hell than balloon heaven, I guess. And I've just about forgot about the how-to part of this essay: How to do your family proud.

I suppose it depends on what part of the family you're talking about. I ain't heard from daddy for a long time, so I don't know if he thinks I'm doing the family proud or not. And Mamma, well Mamma keeps telling me that I should just hang in there, that I didn't do nothing wrong and if I did do something I just done what any boy would do. Any good old boy. My new step-daddy just nods his head up and down when Mamma says that. So I guess that part of my family is right proud of me. And the fellows down at the B&B treated me like I was the local boy made good, buying me drinks and cheering me on.

But Mamaw don't seem proud. She somehow don't see that I made good. She all but said she feels shamed. Shamed. Mamaw ain't one for shame. It makes a body wonder why she can't see what everybody else does. But I guess Mamaw's been my only real family for a long time now. And she has very peculiar ideas on how to do the family proud, ideas I ain't always cottoned to. But I'm tired of running from her.

She's ten years older than the last time I ran from her. That was the same spring vacation when I sassed her in the field about resting easy in the Lord. I sassed her again a day or two later, and that time she didn't just hold her breath and start to sermonizing. She lay down the hoe and started for me. I lay mine down, too, and scooted on up the mountain.

I was a good runner in those days, my legs just bulging with hill muscles and my lungs clean of all that tobacco I've sucked in since and it wasn't any time before I left that old woman way behind.

But she kept coming. I'd sit down on a rock to catch my breath and I could hear her way below, but getting closer. So I'd dash off a ways more, just to keep the distance between us. But she kept coming. No matter how much space I put between that old woman and me, she kept squeezing it tighter. All that afternoon and into the night, I heard Mamaw coming.

Finally, she was right there before me. Neither one of us had any energy left for running, but I knew that wouldn't stop her.

"Son," she said, "are you ready to take your licking?"

"Yes, ma'am," I answered, not seeing any out for it.

"Well," she said, "come on down to the house and I'll get your Papaw to give you one tomorrow."

"Ain't you going to give it to me now?" I said. I had got all prepared and didn't relish waiting.

"I'm too wore out to give a proper one and you need a proper one. You're just going to have to spend the night anticipating." Mamaw always knew anticipating was the worst part of any licking.

"Mamaw," I said on the way down, "why didn't you just wait till I came home if you weren't going to do the licking tonight. You know I'd have to come back eventually."

"That ain't so, son. You might have kept on running. You're old enough and you think you're smart enough. As long as I'm able, I'm going to keep on running after you. I let too much family go. I ain't gonna to let you go if I can help it."

Papaw gave me that licking next day, and it was a good one. Papaw never was one much for licking, but Mamaw urged him some. She couldn't much move from her run the day before, but she sat in the big room and told Papaw to keep at it every time he seemed to be letting off some.

"That boy ain't had enough yet," she'd say, "lay on some more."

Well he lay on till I was moving just about as stiff as she was, which I always suspected was part of her reasoning. I started out determined not to let a sniffle out of me, but after awhile I began to fear that he was going to keep at it, or she was going to keep him at it until they heard a sniffle or two. They might be afraid I wasn't hurting enough. So I let out a cry or two, which wasn't hard by that time, and by and by he stopped.

I think that licking about did Papaw in. He died at the end of that summer, and never did much more of anything after that licking.

Later on that night, Mamaw came over to my bed. I was still hurting some, and mad, too. It hadn't set right, her urging Papaw on like she had. I don't know if she was feeling guilty or not, Mamaw never was one to admit to that kind of thing to anyone let alone her children, but she brung some fresh-baked fritters and a tall glass of milk. I considered not taking it, but I was fourteen, and just about always hungry. She sat by me while I ate and she stroked my head some. Mamaw ain't much giving to that kind of softness and it startled me some.

"Baby boy," she calls me, and I was already six-foot some, "I just wanted you to know that running away always makes things worse. There ain't no punishment so bad that facing it don't cut it in half."

Seems to me that she had doubled it in spite, but I held my peace. I wasn't about to start sassing her again, least ways not till my scars had healed a bit.

"But I want you to know," she continued, "that I'm right proud of the way you took your punishment. You done wrong and you've been punished. But you done me proud the way you stood it."

So I mean to do my family proud again the same way, though I don't suppose anybody's going to be bringing me fresh fritters and milk, or stroking my head. And it will take more than a day or so to shake the aches out of my limbs. I'm older now, and aches don't go away so quick, and I done more than just sass my Mamaw. I done a whole lot more. But I mean to do them proud the only way left I've got to do them proud.

Chapter 22

Hugh's lawyer wasn't happy when Linda showed up with the essay but Hugh admitted writing it and the lawyer couldn't do too much about that. It didn't prove rape, though, the lawyer insisted and he got the charge reduced to sexual abuse. Hugh pleaded guilty. The lawyer shook his head. He'd done his best but his client was a fool. Still, he told Hugh he didn't expect he'd be sentenced to more than a year or two. Behave yourself, he told him, and you'll be out in six months.

Hugh's guilty plea surprised a lot of people but didn't change too many minds. It didn't make sense to some so they made sense out of it their own way. That woman was just poison, and no better than she ought to be. Sexual Abuse as a charge kind of muddied the water. Nobody really knew what it meant but it seemed to many that she was as guilty as he was. More—what with her being the teacher and the drinking and all. Things had just gone further than she wanted or expected and so she turned on the boy. People were disgusted. What a woman can't do to a man's mind.

Jimmy wasn't happy, either. "Six months . If he serves that much." But he was calmer. She felt him calmer, for weeks now, as if he had resolved something in his mind.

They still hadn't made love. It was July. Vines had crawled up their deck and were climbing the banisters. There was a thickness in the air that went beyond humidity. It had just rained, hard, for about five minutes. The thunderstorm had blown up out of nowhere it seemed, dark clouds forming out of clear sky. The moisture in the air whipped to a whirlwind. But then it was gone. The sky was clear again. The rain steamed back to the sky in the heat. And the air was even thicker than it had been. The Kentucky rain forest, she thought.

It was too hot to make love but one look from Jimmy and she would have put that thought aside. She wore a halter and shorts—the Bedouin sweatshirt no longer possible or wanted—but she didn't feel Jimmy looking at her. The Botts boy had come up with her mail and hung around so long she thought she was going to have to feed him dinner. But Jimmy stayed on his corner of the deck, grousing about Hugh. Some things end, she thought, and some are bludgeoned to death. Which was this? She took a bottle of sun lotion and began to rub it slowly over her thighs. She paused.

"Jimmy, rub some on my back."

He looked troubled by her request but pulled himself up and came over to sit behind her on her lounge chair. His legs straddled hers as if they were riding tandem on a bike. He started to rub the oil without warming it and she jumped at the cold. "Sorry," he mumbled and took care to rub his hands together before the next application. He was tentative at first, awkward, as if he were afraid to touch her. But he pressed deeper as he went on, his rhythm steadier. She scooted her bottom closer to his legs. He was wearing running shorts and with her fingertips she began to rub the hairs of his legs against the grain. She heard his sharp intake of breath. She reached around with her fingers and pinched the under flesh of his thighs, the only soft spots on Jimmy's legs. She snuggled even closer and felt the soft nest of his penis harden. She reached with one finger and touched the sac.

Jimmy stopped rubbing. She turned to him, letting the rest of her halter slip away. She pulled his face down into her breasts. His thumbs hooked onto her shorts and stripped them from her. "Jimmy," she called as he yanked off his own shorts and hovered above her for a moment—a last hesitation—"Jimmy," she called again as she felt him push all the way in—all the way into her as she looked up at the vines swaying in the July haze that surrounded her.

"They offered me a contract," she said. Jimmy nodded as if that was to be expected, but she had been surprised. It must have been Jeanette's doing—or maybe Tom Black's. Nobody else wanted her to stay, except perhaps her one new friend among the secretaries. She had begun sending Linda little notes. She had typed up the latest evaluations and sent them on. "Some real good ones there," said her friend, though the school had begun to implement the fiction that the secretaries didn't read what they typed. Linda thumbed the package of evaluations in front of her, afraid to read them for all her friend's encouragement even though she knew that many of the students who most hated her had dropped before evaluations. "That's the trick, honey," Kerry told her. "Get them out before they get you out."

"I don't always understand her, but I think she's a good teacher."

That was fair. Who always understood anybody? She looked over at Jimmy. He had decided to plant tomatoes though it was way too late in the season and they didn't get enough sun anyway. "It's not too late," he insisted. "It just means we might have some green ones left over. It's never too late" and he struck at a clod of dirt as hard as a rock. She looked back at the evaluation. She didn't always understand them, so they were even. They probably had understood her more than she had them. "Balloon heaven." She laughed and was surprised at her laugh.

"After great pain a formal feeling comes." Emily got it right as usual. But the formal feeling was going and she could laugh.

"Miss Eliot is the best English teacher I ever had."

Well, that was nice. She wondered what the competition had been. She was certainly the most talked about English teacher anybody had ever had. Around here.

"I didn't learn anything the whole semester except for a lot of personal things about her I could have lived without."

Amen to that. She could have lived without them, too. Jimmy had paused in his hoeing. "How about a beer?"

"Sure," she shouted back. "Make mine a light." She laughed again as she struggled to her feet and padded barefoot to the refrigerator. She wondered at her good mood. "Didn't learn anything the whole semester." That was hard to believe. Who went a whole semester without learning something? She sure hadn't.

"Then the letting go." That was the end of the poem. She hadn't let go yet, but she could laugh. That was something.

"Should I sign it?" she asked, handing Jimmy his beer. He looked surprised.

"That's up to you. You feel comfortable going back? We can go anywhere."

Comfortable. Who was comfortable ? Was she comfortable in the Bronx? Would she be comfortable working with Kerry again? Did they even want her back? She turned to the house. The slant had gotten worse. You had to cock your head sideways to see the A. Her landlords wanted her to stay, that's for sure. She'd be sorry to leave the house at least.

"Go anywhere." The world was all before them, where to choose. Jimmy was comfortable with her again. Could Hugh come back, she wondered, if she stayed? Mamaw still had the land. He could come back for that. She wished she could see Mamaw or at least hear about her. She wished she could visit Mamaw while Hugh was in jail. Mamaw would welcome her. Put her to work like Sister. But she didn't think she could go back there.

"You can't be letting people run you out just cause they don't like you." Caroline had been firm. "Good heavens, think of Margaret. Do you think Margaret gives a hoot's eye if people care for her or not. She just does her job. There'll be plenty of people to appreciate that. And I'm not exactly Miss Popularity myself. That's why I hooked up with Sister so people wouldn't notice that much. But when I move they're going to be carrying me."

"Jimmy says we can go anywhere."

"That just means he'd go anywhere with you. Not that he wants to. That boy'd follow you back to the Bronx. He's got it bad." And Caroline laughed. Back to the Bronx. What could be worse than that?

"You just hang in there, Miss Eliot. Don't let what people say get you down." A few of the evaluations had offered advice—as if her situation had called for a reversal in roles between teacher and student. She felt grateful. Hang in there. It seemed everybody's favorite suggestion. Hang in there. Jimmy had filed for a new judge in the house case and it looked like he was going to get one. The company was mumbling about increasing the offer. Just hang in there.

"And then what? What if next year's as bad as this one?"

"What if it is? Though it's not likely to be the same. Next year's bad will be different." Caroline already had tomatoes on her vines. Not ripe yet but coming along. "Wait till you taste the tomato juice that will come out of this. Sweeter than anything you've ever had. No tang at all."

"Your mamma must have told you there's no life-time guarantees. Or your daddy. We don't have all the wisdom down South—some of it must have dribbled up North. Even that boy who thinks you're the best thing since sliced cheese might change his mind. It happens. Don't look like that. I didn't say it was going to happen. I don't expect it to happen. But it could."

It could. Jimmy was heading into a shower. He smiled as he passed her. "Want to join me?" It didn't seem likely but it could happen though living with him full-time hadn't cooled his libido yet. She shook her head at him. She had to think. Think. Whatever that was. The trees almost brushed the windows and the vines were taking over. It was like living in a greenhouse. The whole hollow was like living in a greenhouse. Did she want to stay?

She did. For a while. One more year at least. This year she'd do better. She could hardly do worst. Besides, she wanted to see the Fall flowers. She'd been too busy to look the year before. Caroline claimed they were as pretty as the Spring's.

"Prettier," said Sister who Linda had never heard express an opinion about flowers one way or another.

The evaluations lay before her. She had read enough. Enough evaluating. Enough judging. She wasn't very good at it. That was obvious. She closed her eyes and let it all go. Or as much as she could let go. She didn't feel as worried anymore. She didn't feel as afraid. It didn't matter as much. Jimmy was yelling for something—-soap or towel. It didn't matter what it was exactly, she knew it was her he was really yelling for. It was her he wanted—close to him. So close to him.

She kept her eyes closed for a few moments more, feeling the deep sweet rest that seemed to come only in those moments before she knew she'd have to move, those last seconds in the morning before rising. But she opened her eyes at last and she was glad to do so. She blinked. The long summer evening was almost over, the sun just a peak of light above her mountain. Her mountain. Filled with second growth trees in full summer bloom.

Jimmy was still yelling. "Add some cold water to that steam," she shouted out as she went to join him.

Printed in the United States
40938LVS00006B/346-396

9 781893 239456